DAD

"I want to tell Holly who you are."

Drew waited for Karen's reaction.

"No!" Karen almost choked on the word. "You can't. For heaven's sake, what will it do to her?"

"Nothing as drastic as your desertion ten years ago."

"What on earth," she said fiercely, "will be gained by telling her at this late stage that she has a mother?"

"She knows that, Karen. She just doesn't know where her mother is. She accepted it well. Only lately she's been...unhappy about it. For a ten-year-old girl a mother is important. She needs someone, Karen."

Mentally Karen braced herself. "I suppose you have someone in mind?" She wouldn't have believed that this could hurt so much.

He was staring at her strangely. "Yes," he said slowly, "I have someone in mind."

DAPHNE CLAIR, a fourth-generation New Zealander, lives with her family of five in the subtropical area known as "The Winterless North." In addition to her contemporary romances, she writes poetry, historical novels under various names and has won literary prizes for her short stories. About three times a year she tutors courses to help other writers develop their craft. She says she hates windy days, shopping, daylight saving time, prickly plants and having her photograph taken.

Books by Daphne Clair

HARLEQUIN PRESENTS

HARLEQUIN ROMANCE

DAPHNE CLAIR

no escape

Harlequin Books

TORONTO • NEW YORK • LONDON
AMSTERDAM • PARIS • SYDNEY • HAMBURG
STOCKHOLM • ATHENS • TOKYO • MILAN

Harlequin Presents first edition March 1988
ISBN 0-373-11056-1

Original hardcover edition published in 1987
by Mills & Boon Limited

CHAPTER ONE

THE coffee bar was very crowded. The noise of clattering china and clacking tongues seemed to be inside her head, and the faint, dull pounding at her temples was intensifying. She hesitated by the pile of plates and the stacked trays on the shelf below them, at the entrance to the chrome corral that always reminded her of a cattle race. She was tempted to skip lunch and return to the relative quiet of the boutique. But the headache would only get worse if she didn't eat, and already a tall man in a dark suit was standing in her peripheral vision, waiting for her to move on. Even seen from the corner of her eye, his stance suggested impatience. Without enthusiasm she picked up a thick, warmed, china plate and moved into the narrow space before the rows of sandwiches and savouries and sticky, cream-filled cakes.

Just a sandwich or two, she thought, and a cup of tea. Perhaps she ought to have a tray to make carrying them easier. She half turned and bent to get one, just as the man who had moved up beside her made to do the same, and their shoulders collided. His was solid beneath the lightweight wool suiting, and she winced at the impact.

'*Oh!* Sorry!' she gasped, straightening up. Then her heart lurched sickeningly and her eyes dilated in shock. 'Drew!'

He seemed broader and taller than she remembered, and there were faint lines about his eyes that had not been there ten years ago. His mouth, firmly closed after a cursory apology of his own, looked almost grim, and his mahogany-coloured hair had been cut shorter than before. But she would have known him anywhere.

The cobalt-blue gaze he turned on her was cool, a

puzzled frown starting to form between his brows as he said, 'I'm sorry, I don't——'

She saw the sudden jolt of recognition in his face before he made a lightning, disbelieving assessment of her, taking in the sleekly drawn back, honey-blonde hair; the expert make-up complementing her brown eyes under fine brows and emphasising high cheekbones and the soft outline of her mouth; the cream real silk blouse and champagne-coloured linen skirt and jacket; even her expensive Italian shoes. His gaze returned to her face and he said with stunned softness, '*Karen*?'

She wished she hadn't said his name. He had hardly looked at her until then, and probably wouldn't have recognised her at all. But it was too late to deny her identity. Already he was recovering from his first surprise, the certainty in his face belying the questioning note in his voice. He shook his head as if to clear it, and looked at her again, more slowly, his eyes narrowing as he took in the changes, comparing the lank-haired, carelessly dressed girl he had known with the *soignée*, mature version he saw before him now. But all he said was, 'You're thinner.'

Someone said loudly, 'Excuse me!' They had been too absorbed to notice the queue of people forming behind him. He glanced at the plump middle-aged woman nudging at his elbow, and turned back to Karen. 'We can't talk here,' he said. Taking the plate from her hand and returning it to the shelf, he gripped her arm firmly and, ignoring the curious stares they were attracting, took her with him out of the enclosure and propelled her across to the door.

It wasn't until they were nearly there that she recovered herself sufficiently to resist his hold, saying, 'We really don't have anything to talk about, do we?'

He reached round her to open the door. 'You don't think so?' he said with deadly sarcasm. 'It's been ten years, Karen. I'd say we have a fair bit of catching up to do.'

He almost shoved her outside into the street and she blinked in the weak spring sunshine. Pulling away from his hand, she stepped back with an instinctive desire to put some distance between them, narrowly missing a collision with a pedestrian hurrying past, who skirted her adroitly and cast her a look of exasperation. 'There's nothing to say,' she insisted coldly, regaining her poise.

'*My God, you've got a nerve!*' His voice slashed at her. He grabbed at her arm again and began walking rapidly, forcing her to go along unless she wanted to create a scene in the crowded, narrow street.

'What do you think you're doing?' she demanded in a furious undertone.

'Finding somewhere we can talk!' He hesitated at the edge of the pavement to let a car go by, then proceeded across the road at a pace that made her breathless. 'We'll go to the park,' he said.

'I don't want to go to the park! I don't want to go anywhere with you!'

He looked down at her, and she almost shivered at the blatant hostility in his eyes. '*Shut up,*' he said between his teeth. 'If you think I'm going to just calmly watch you walk away, you must be more of a fool than I ever imagined.'

As they reached the kerb she stopped suddenly and tried to jerk her arm from his hold. He said nothing, but his mouth set in a hard line, and his fingers intensified their grip until it was painful. He said, 'I'm not letting you go, Karen. Come on.'

'I could scream.'

'You could. Someone might call the police. Are you willing to explain the situation to them?'

'I'll simply say I've never seen you before in my life.'

'There were plenty of witnesses in the coffee bar to swear that you came with me willingly.'

'*Willingly?*'

'Stop quibbling. You didn't start a fuss then, it's a bit

late to do it now. You'd only make a fool of yourself, and you know it.'

She looked at him defiantly, telling herself she ought to make a fuss, anyway. Scream, ask a passer-by for help, simply refuse to move so that he would have to drag her if he wanted her to go a step further. But the circumstances didn't call for such histrionics. He was right. She wouldn't only embarrass him, she would embarrass herself horribly, and she wasn't the type to relish making a spectacle of herself in public.

As if he sensed her capitulation, Drew subtly altered the pressure on her arm, urging her forward, and reluctantly she took a step and stiffly resumed walking beside him. In silence they climbed the steps that led into the leafy sanctuary of Albert Park, and walked up one of the steep paths until the gothic spire of the University tower was visible through the branches of the trees. Drew steered her across the grass to the shade of an exotic old tree with furled green leaves beginning to dress its bare branches, and pushed her down on to a wooden seat, his arm resting on its back as he sat a couple of feet away and turned towards her.

She was breathing quickly; he had walked them uphill without a break in his stride, and in her high heels she had found it difficult to keep up, but wouldn't ask him to slow down.

'You're out of condition,' he remarked, watching the rise and fall of her blouse with hard, disparaging eyes. 'It isn't exercise that's made you lose weight.'

She cast him a look of disbelief. 'Did you bring me up here to discuss the state of my health?'

'You know better than that,' he said curtly. Then, his glance holding something she couldn't read, he said, 'But while we're on the subject ... how are you? All right?'

Karen suppressed a strong desire to laugh. After ten years, it was such a banal question. Now that he had coerced her into accepting his determination to talk to her, this was all he could think of to say? Next, she supposed, he would be remarking on the weather.

Meantime, he seemed to be waiting for an answer.

'Of course I'm all right,' she said, just stopping herself from returning the query. He looked well. Older, of course, and also more sure of himself. Not that he had ever been diffident. At twenty-two, he had had the air of a young man who was going places. Now he was obviously a man who had arrived. He was even more attractive than when she had first fallen head over heels in love with him, although the last trace of the boyishness which had been part of his charm had entirely disappeared.

'Then why so much thinner?' he asked. 'Have you been dieting?'

'I wish you'd stop harping on the subject!' she snapped. 'It may have escaped your notice at the time, but I was actually overweight when I ... when you last saw me. I was hardly old enough to have lost my puppy fat, and then ...'

He grinned faintly, but his eyes weren't smiling. 'You never had any puppy fat. You were always gorgeous.'

The casual compliment took her unawares. For a moment she was shaken with a piercing nostalgia. To cover it, she said bitingly, 'I'm sorry if my looks no longer meet with your approval. But it hardly matters now, does it?'

The slight curve that had softened his mouth disappeared abruptly. 'Obviously not.' All the same, he couldn't seem to stop looking at her. His hostile eyes travelled over her again, resting momentarily on the slim gold watch she wore on her left wrist. He seemed to find something particularly distasteful about it, and she shifted restlessly. 'What are you doing with yourself these days?' he asked.

'I'm doing all right,' she said evasively.

With deceptive patience, he said, 'Yes, we've already established that. Who bought you the watch?'

For a moment she was simply astonished at the question, before her brain supplied her with the reason for it. '*I* bought it!' she said. 'With my own money, that I earned myself.'

His brows rose. 'Well, bully for you! There's no need to be so defensive about it. Have you turned into a raving feminist, darling?'

'Don't call me that!'

'Darling? Why not?'

Because she didn't like the way he had said it, with so different an inflection from the tenderness of ten years ago ...

Aloud she said, 'It isn't ... relevant any more, is it?' She looked down at her hands, clutching her imported leather bag.

'Relevant!' He repeated the word with derision. 'So what would you call relevant?' He picked up her left hand suddenly, his fingers warm and hard as they held her wrist. She suppressed an instinct to snatch it away. 'No ring,' he said. 'I suppose that's irrelevant, too.'

'It ... yes,' she agreed, feeling sick. The headache was getting worse, a definite thumping now, and unlikely to go away.

'What did you do with it?' he asked with seeming carelessness. 'Pawn it?'

Karen shook her head. 'Drew, this isn't getting us anywhere. Please ... let's forget the whole thing.' She made to tug her hand from his hold, and he met her eyes, his fingers slowly tightening, until her teeth clenched in an effort not to protest, then just as slowly he let go.

'I thought that's what you had done,' he said. 'Only for me, you see, it wasn't so easy.'

'I know. I'm ... sorry.'

'*Sorry!*' He leaned towards her, his eyes dark and full of barely contained rage. 'That's hardly adequate ...'

'I *know* that!' She put a hand to her temple, trying to smooth away the ache. 'I know I can never explain to you, but ...'

'*Try me*,' he interrupted harshly.

Karen shook her head, and winced, wishing she hadn't. 'It's no use,' she said. 'It's all water under the bridge. Let it go, Drew. Please.'

'No way!' he said violently. 'What do you think I am, Karen? I looked for you for months—years. I've never really stopped. I'd be walking down a street in a strange town, and some girl would turn a corner and something about her hair, or the way she walked . . . I'd go running after her. And it was never you.'

She raised both her hands this time and dropped her throbbing head on them.

'What's the matter?' Drew said, his voice jeering, totally unsympathetic. 'Am I upsetting you? I hope so. I hope to God I am!'

'Drew, *don't*!'

'Why not?' He grasped both her wrists this time, hauling them away from her face, turning her roughly so that she had to look at him. 'You put me through hell,' he said. 'Why shouldn't you suffer a little for it?'

'I didn't do it to hurt you,' she said.

'Oh, no, of course not!' His mouth twisted bitterly. 'I don't suppose you gave a thought to what it would do to me . . . or anyone else. The only person you thought about at all was yourself.'

'That's not true!'

'Then tell me what is!' he invited, but the sneer in his voice made it impossible to accept. 'Tell me it wasn't because you were a selfish, immature little bitch who simply couldn't accept responsibility, and so you just decided to opt for freedom and a good time.'

'It wasn't like that!'

'Well, *how was it*?' His hands shifted to her shoulders, and she knew he was within an inch of shaking her. 'Go on . . . tell me about it.'

'I can't talk to you like this,' she said. 'You don't want to listen. You just want to hurt me.'

His eyes narrowed as she held them with hers, willing

him to bring his temper under control. He took a deep breath, steadying himself. 'Damn right I do,' he said. His fingers dug into her flesh through her dress.

Then abruptly she was free, and he turned on the seat, leaning forward with his elbows on his knees, his fingers linked as if he needed to do that to keep his hands off her. 'I have an almost overwhelming desire to strangle you. I thought I'd got over that, along with the pain and the grief. But seeing you ... has brought it all back.'

Karen took a shaken breath. 'I'm sorry. I didn't expect to meet you. Are you ... are you visiting Auckland?'

He turned and gave her a curious, probing look. 'No,' he said. 'We're living here now. I'm working for the Board of Overseas Trade and Development.'

She wasn't sure if it was the 'we' or the fact that he had moved to the same city as herself that had jolted her unpleasantly.

'It sounds important,' she said, tritely.

His brows lifted, and for a moment she thought he was going to say something cutting. Instead, he said, 'I like to think so. I'm in charge and I have a free hand in my department. I find it interesting. And you?' he asked, with the politeness of a stranger, but overlaid with sarcasm.

For a panicky moment she contemplated lying. But there was no point. 'I've been living here for a long time,' she said. 'Years.'

'Ten,' he supplied, cynicism twisting his mouth.

She didn't deny it. When she had fled the small Southland town where she had first met Drew on her very last school holiday, she had made for the furthest, biggest city available to her in New Zealand, putting the wind-tossed, watery barrier of Cook Strait and almost the entire length of the country between them.

'You must have changed your name,' he said. As she looked at him warily, he added, 'Yes, I made enquiries ... as far as I could.'

'It isn't illegal to use another name. Except for criminal purposes.'

'I know. And you weren't technically a missing person, since you left of your own free will. The police weren't much help. I expect they thought I beat you.'

She gave him a quick, nervous look, and he nodded grimly. 'It wasn't comfortable, but there were worse things.' His eyes returned to her face.

She didn't want to hear about the worse things. She didn't want to ask the question that she knew he was waiting for. Instead she said, 'I don't know about you, but I have to get back to work.' She stood up, holding her bag firmly in one hand.

'And where's that?' He was standing, too, looking down at her.

Again she thought he was bigger than she remembered, his shoulders seemed broader. 'In the city.'

He smiled rather unpleasantly, his eyes gimlet sharp. 'You may as well tell me,' he said. 'I've no intention of just letting you disappear out of my life again.'

'It's better,' she said, pleading with her eyes.

'The hell it is! I have questions for you that I've been saving up for ten years. And you're going to damn well answer them!'

Fear sent a shiver down her spine. 'No!' she said, her voice low, her eyes sliding away from him, instinctively looking for an escape route.

'Oh, yes,' he said implacably. '*Yes, and yes and yes!* You don't get away that easily. Not this time. Where do you work?'

She shut her lips stubbornly, staring at the grey and blue silk tie he wore. She was unprepared for his sudden snatch at her bag, her fingers much too late as she tried to re-establish her grip on the leather. She grabbed at his arm as he turned from her and opened the catch. 'Give that back!' she cried furiously.

'In a minute.' Coolly, he rifled the contents, found her cheque book, bank passbook and a small pack of her business cards. He glanced at the bank books and slipped them back in the bag, then gave her a look of surprised speculation before extracting one of the lavender-edged cards naming her as Karena Lacey, proprietor of Lavender and Lace, and describing the boutique as 'specialising in fine undergarments made to exclusive designs' and giving the address in one of the inner city shopping arcades.

'*Undergarments?*' His voice held laughter, and she flushed with annoyance. 'Why not go the whole hog and call it Lacey Lingerie?'

'I thought it was too obvious,' she said icily.

'Then why choose Lacey for a name?'

'It was my grandmother's maiden name.'

'Of course. And you don't think that's "obvious"? I must admit it worked, though. I wasn't able to trace it.' He tucked the card into his breast pocket and handed back her bag.

'Give me that card!' she said.

He smiled. 'Don't be silly. I've memorised the address anyway. So I'll keep this ...' his fingers covered the pocket for a moment '... as a memento.'

Defeated, Karen decided to make one more try. 'Drew,' she said, 'this is doing neither of us any good. Please, won't you reconsider? Just tear it up and forget you ever met me again. It's been so long ... we're two different people. You can't still love me ...'

'Who said anything about loving you?' he asked callously.

Unexpectedly, that hurt. It was a moment before she could speak again, and her voice was husky. 'Then what can you possibly want from me?'

'I told you. Answers. And I'm going to get them.'

'It's no *use!*' she cried.

'We'll see.'

'Drew, I've made a whole new life for myself ... so have you. What's the point of dragging up the past? It's over.'

'Is it? Aren't you forgetting something?'

His eyes accused her, a cold fury raging in their depths. A stab of pain attacked her temples, and she felt them go icy and moist. Memories beat at her brain, memories she had spent years trying to forget. *No!* her mind howled. *Please no!* Dumbly, she shook her head.

'*You haven't even asked!*' he said with harsh contempt.

She pushed past him, stumbling on the grass as her heels sank into the soft earth. She had to get away. He was breaking her, forcing her to think about the unthinkable, bringing to the surface a pain so acute that she could not have gone on living without burying it as deeply as she was able, not allowing herself ever to have time to entertain it.

The terrible need to know was beating in her brain. But she wouldn't ask. She wouldn't! All these years she had suppressed the unbearable curiosity, the constant irrational fear, the imagined disasters. Only last night she had wakened sweating and trembling from another nightmare of violence, pain and death.

Drew had the power to assuage that dreadful, nagging anxiety, to keep the nightmares at bay for a time, at least. Or perhaps to confirm them. The possibility filled her with dread. And with unbearable longing. As her feet found the hardness of the asphalt path, she hesitated and was lost. She had to know.

She took a deep breath, and turned slowly to face him. He was coming towards her, stopping only an arm's length away, his gaze accusing, judging and condemning her.

She told herself to be calm, schooling her face to show no emotion. But her voice croaked in her throat, barely audible. 'How ... is she?'

He had one hand in his pocket, his stance apparently relaxed, but his face was a granite mask. His black brows lifted. A cruel mockery lacing his voice, he said, 'How is who?'

She gasped a silent, stricken protest, her mouth

opening on a sharp breath, her head thudding with a
loud hammer beat. She was going to cry, or scream, or
faint. Her eyes begged for mercy, for at least the
kindness of putting her out of her suspense, as she tried
to form words, and couldn't, her lips trembling on all
the questions she had asked herself unanswerably for ten
years.

Blindly she turned away from him and fled down the
smooth path, heedless of its steepness and her unsuitable
shoes. She was half-way down when she realised that
the momentum of her speed was dangerous, and tried to
stop. It wasn't possible. She felt her ankle turn with a
wrenching agony, and then went crashing headlong to
the ground.

Drew was the first to reach her, although other people
gathered round. She felt dizzy and sick and her whole
body was sore, and for a few moments the world
mercifully retreated in a haze of blackness. Then Drew
was lifting her to lean on his shoulder, his hands
amazingly gentle. He said, 'Where does it hurt?'

'Everywhere,' she mumbled. 'My ankle ... is it
broken?'

Through a haze of pain and a babble of strange voices
she heard him say to someone, 'Get a taxi. I'll take her to
the hospital.' His fingers touched her ankle and she
yelped.

'Sorry, darling,' he murmured, and something
brushed her forehead softly. He can't have kissed me,
she thought, he doesn't love me any more, he just said
so. 'My hand,' she said, becoming conscious of a
separate discomfort. 'It stings.'

He opened her fingers, and said, 'You've grazed it
quite badly. Here.' A soft wad of linen was pressed into
her palm, and she looked down and saw that it was a
folded handkerchief, and that her blood was soaking into
it.

'I'll spoil it,' she said.

'Never mind.'

'I feel awful.'

'I know. Don't worry. I don't think anything's broken, but we'll take you up to casualty at the hospital and make sure.'

She felt she ought to tell him not to bother, but she did feel sick, and talking seemed to make it worse. So she closed her eyes and let her head rest against him. After a little while he said, 'I'm going to carry you to the taxi. I'll try not to hurt you.'

She nodded with an effort, and gritted her teeth as he swung her into his arms. He got her into the back seat, dropped her bag into her lap, and sat with his arm about her.

'Thank you,' she said weakly. 'It's very good of you.'

He didn't answer, and she missed seeing the look that he threw her, because she had closed her eyes again.

At the hospital they cleaned up grazes on her left hand and on the knuckles of the other, and a scrape on her elbow that she hadn't even noticed, and bandaged the ankle, assuring her it was only a bad sprain that rest and cold compresses would soon cure. Twice she suggested that Drew should go, but he refused. 'I'll take you home,' he said when it was all over.

'No, really, you've done enough.'

'That's an understatement,' he said, under his breath.

Surprised, she looked at him quickly. 'It wasn't your fault.'

He didn't answer, but his look was sceptical.

'You're not responsible for me. I'm sure you have things to do.' Her voice was stronger, almost crisp.

'Feeling better, are you?' He sounded sarcastic.

She was still sore and stiff, and her headache hadn't improved either, but she wasn't dizzy any more and she could think relatively clearly. 'Yes,' she said. 'So you can quite safely leave me to find my own way home.'

'I've already phoned for another taxi.'

'I'll pay you back for the fares.'

'You'll do nothing of the sort.'

Karen didn't have the strength to argue.

He sent the cab away when it deposited them outside her townhouse. 'I'll be all right now, thank you,' she said, trying to sound firm.

'You look like death,' he told her tersely. He put an arm about her waist, and she was, weakly, glad to lean on it. 'Did they give you anything to take, at the hospital?'

'Some pain relievers and a sedative, in case I need them,' she said. And she did need them, she thought, as she eased away from him to lean against the wall of the little porch, and fumbled for her key.

He took it from her and opened the door and helped her into the tiled entry-way. She stumbled, and he caught her, lifting her up in his arms and said, 'You'd better lie down. Where's the bedroom?'

'I have to phone the boutique,' she said. 'My assistant will be worried.'

'I'll do it. Your bedroom?' he reiterated.

Karen gave in. 'Upstairs.'

Fortunately the stairwell was quite wide, with a good turn half-way up. He didn't knock her ankle, and he was scarcely panting at all when he deposited her on the wide bed with the cream crochet cover over an amber taffeta underlay.

'Very feminine,' he commented, looking round at the cream lace curtains, the Queen Anne dressing-table and the deep-pile dyed-wool rugs in shades of gold and amber. 'Do you want the cover off the bed?'

'I'll do it.'

He cast her an exasperated glance and began to remove the cover, helping her to shift over on the bed so that he could take it right off, and folding it carefully before placing it on the stool before the dressing-table. He came back to the bed and removed her shoes and put them down on the floor. 'You don't have a phone in here?' he asked.

'No. I hate being woken up by a telephone ringing in my ear. It's downstairs in the kitchen.'

'I'll phone the shop for you, and make you a cup of tea. Anything else you'd like?'

'No, thanks. A cup of tea will do.'

'You had no lunch.' His fault, she thought, but didn't say so.

'It's all right. I'm not hungry.'

He hesitated. 'You should change into something you can rest in comfortably.'

'Something clean, you mean?' Her clothes were smudged with dirt and blood.

'That, too. Do you want me to help you to the bathroom? Shall I get some clothes out for you?'

'I can get them. And I'll manage the bathroom, too. Please ... I'd rather.'

'There's not much point in being coy with me.'

She gritted her teeth. 'I'm not being coy. Please ring the boutique. Gretta will be going spare.'

When he had gone, she hobbled into the bathroom, had a quick wash, a little awkwardly because her left hand was bandaged, and discarded her soiled clothes, placing them in the basket in the corner. Her slip had escaped the accident, she noted thankfully. It was one she had made herself, of fine primrose lawn trimmed with a particularly dainty broderie and very narrow palest primrose ribbon.

Her head was full of little men with large sledge-hammers, and she pulled out the pins that held a hairstyle decidedly the worse for wear, experiencing a momentary relief as the tightly confined strands were freed to fall down her back. In the bedroom, she picked up the tortoiseshell hairbrush off the dressing-table before sinking gratefully on to the bed and pulling up the sheet.

When Drew came in carrying a tray with a cup of tea and a plate of biscuits on it, she was propped up on the pillow, tiredly but determinedly brushing her hair.

'Do you need to do that?' he asked.

Her hand dropped. 'If I don't it will be unmanageable

in the morning.' Her hair was fine and straight, inclined to go into rats' tails easily, and tangled badly if she slept with it loose. Every night she brushed it thoroughly and braided it into a loose plait.

'You've changed the colour,' Drew said, putting the tray down on the bedside table.

'Not really,' she said, instantly defensive. She used a highlighting shampoo, but the change from the lank, mousy tresses he remembered was mostly brought about by frequent washing with a properly formulated shampoo, the right type of conditioner and nightly attention with a good soft-bristled brush.

'Drink your tea while it's hot. I put in one and half of sugar. OK?'

She picked up the cup. 'Yes.' For some reason it shook her that he still remembered. 'Would you pass my bag over, please?' It was on the dressing-table. 'I think I'll take some of those pills. What did Gretta say?'

'She's sorry about the accident, don't worry about a thing, and she'll call round tonight on her way home to see if you need anything. She said she can use the spare key you keep at the shop to let herself in. Your Gretta seems very efficient. I shouldn't think you need to be too concerned about the shop.'

Swallowing down two pills with the tea, Karen replied, 'No, she's very good. I'm lucky to have her. What did you tell her?' Drew raised his brows, and she added, hating him for making her spell it out, 'Did you say who you were?'

'I told her my name. It didn't mean a thing to her.'

'No, it wouldn't.' She avoided the sardonic look he was giving her, and said, 'I suppose she was surprised . . . a stranger phoning her. Did she think you were a Good Samaritan who picked me up by the wayside?'

'She assumed that you'd been lunching with me.'

Well, that was all right, she thought. Lunch dates were rare for her, but Gretta wouldn't pry, though she might be curious.

'Is there anyone else?' Drew asked; and when she looked at him uncomprehendingly, elucidated, 'Anyone else you'd like me to ring?'

Karen shook her head, making it give a sudden savage throb. She put her hand up to it, and he said, 'What's the matter?'

'My head hurts.'

His voice sharpened. 'Did you hit it when you fell?'

'No, I had a headache already. It's got quite a lot worse, though, with all the ... drama.'

There was a short pause before he said, 'Not surprising, I suppose. It's been a somewhat traumatic day for me, too, but you've certainly got the worst of it.'

The ghost of a wry smile touched her mouth as she put down the empty cup on the saucer and handed them to him. 'Well, you've got some of your own back then, haven't you? Isn't that what you wanted?'

'I didn't intend you to get physically injured!'

He looked rather white about the mouth, and she said, 'I know. Forget I said it.'

'You're rather strong on forgetting things, aren't you?'

She looked away from him, her mouth drooping.

His voice decidedly clipped, he said, 'That wasn't in the Queensberry Rules, was it? You're not in a fit state at the moment.'

'Actually, I'm feeling better by the minute,' she said drowsily. She picked up the brush again and managed a few unsteady strokes over her hair. The brush seemed very heavy in her hand, and the room wavered in front of her eyes.

'Why don't you leave that?'

'I told you,' she sighed.

The brush was taken from her hand and he sat beside her on the bed, his hand unexpectedly gentle on her shoulder as he pushed her into a sitting position. 'Here,' he said. 'Let me.'

She knew she shouldn't, but protest was beyond her.

And the firm strokes were pleasantly sensuous, making her sleepy. He finished and laid her back against the pillow, and her eyelids fluttered in an effort to stay open. 'You're very good,' she said, 'at this sort of thing, aren't you?'

'I've had some practice,' he answered evenly, 'with cuts and scratches ... and brushing a little girl's hair.'

Her eyes were glazing over with the drugs that were beginning to take effect, but she blinked and cleared them for a moment, long enough to say slowly, 'Please, Drew ... how is she?'

His face hardened. 'Why can't you say her name? Have you *forgotten* it?'

It was a moment before the taunt reached her increasingly fuzzy mind. Then she frowned, and moved her head fretfully in negation. He could hardly hear the whispered words. 'No! Don't you understand, Drew?'

'Understand what?'

Her eyes were closed, and she didn't answer. He thought she had gone to sleep, and made to pick up the tray.

Then she moved slightly again, turning her head towards him, and murmured, 'It ... hurts too much.'

He stiffened, then bent towards the bed, his voice urgent. 'What hurts?' he asked. '*Karen?* What hurts too much? Your ankle?'

A faint frown appeared between the delicate curves of her brows. Her head moved on the pillow just a fraction, from side to side.

'Holly!' she whimpered, and a tear slid on to the white linen pillow-slip.

His breath inhaled sharply, and he fell to one knee by the bed. His hands touched her face, holding it between them, willing her to open her eyes again and look at him. 'Karen,' he said. '*Karen!*'

There was no response, not even a flicker of her closed eyelids. 'Karen!' He dipped his head frustratedly, fighting a temptation to shake her into awareness. Then he put his mouth close to her ear, his cheek brushing the smoothness of hers, and said distinctly, 'Karen. She's fine. Holly's fine. She's a lovely little girl, pretty and bright and ... mostly she's happy. Karen?'

Her breathing was light and even, and the pale hair spilled over the pillow was soft and shining. He touched it, stroked back a wayward strand from her cheek, and stood up. He went to the window and stood there for a long time leaning against the frame, looking at the woman sleeping in the bed, his mouth hard, and his eyes baffled. At last he ran a hand through his thick hair, and flexed the muscles of his shoulders, then picked up the tray quietly before leaving the room.

CHAPTER TWO

GRETTA called in early next morning, tied on a pink apron that enhanced her dusky apricot complexion—although it hardly went with the low-necked, frilled crimson blouse and slim, black ankle-length skirt she was wearing—then made Karen some breakfast and helped her downstairs to the sofa in the small, sunny lounge.

'I don't know if this is such a good idea,' she said, as she dropped a rug over Karen's legs. 'Supposing you need the bathroom?'

'There's an extra toilet off the laundry, remember?' Karen reminded her. 'And at least here I can hobble to the kitchen, so I won't starve. I refuse to stay in bed all day. And my work table is here.'

'You're supposed to rest that foot. Don't you dare start working!'

'Gretta, I might as well. I can still use my hands.'

Gretta sighed, resting closed fists on her curvaceous hips, the gold hoops in her ears swinging disapprovingly as she shook her gleaming black head, surmounted by a red and gold ornamental comb. Her ancestry was Samoan, Maori and Swedish, and she had inherited a legacy of striking good looks that put Karen in mind of a gypsy queen. 'You already work all the hours God sends,' she said. 'You'd think you'd be glad to put your feet up for a change and read a good book or something.'

'I've read quite a lot of good books lately,' Karen said. 'I do my reading in bed, at night.'

Gretta grinned, showing splendid teeth, and rolled her dark eyes. 'Can't you think of anything better to do in bed? By the way, who was the dishy feller you were having lunch with yesterday?'

'What makes you think he was dishy?' Karen asked, playing for time.

'He sounded like it, on the phone.'

'Voices can be deceptive.'

'You mean he isn't like his voice?'

Karen shrugged. '*You* might think so. Gretta, the table has wheels. Do me a favour and bring it over here, and I promise not to stir from this spot.'

Gretta sighed, and reluctantly obeyed. 'But not the sewing machine,' she said firmly, depositing it on the floor. 'You can do your drawing and hand sewing if you like, but you can't use *that* without putting your foot on the floor.'

The antique kauri table with slim, turned legs was quite small, but the shallow drawers under the top and the small castors on which it moved made it particularly useful. A roomy old-fashioned work-basket sat on the golden patina of the top, and a half-finished garment was folded carefully beside the basket. The drawers held pencils, and sketch pads and samples of materials which she might use in fresh designs. When Gretta had left, Karen picked up the nightgown on to which she was fixing a frill of hand-made lace, and began painstakingly setting stitches.

Usually she found this kind of activity soothing. Most of the things sold at the boutique were sewn by machine, some by a few selected outworkers who could be relied on to produce consistently good quality work, but Karen liked to add hand-sewn trimmings to them, making each just slightly different from the others. It was a hallmark which made her merchandise sought after by those who were in the know. Sometimes it was merely a matter of a few seconds fixing a tiny bow to the front of a bodice or quickly embroidering a flower motif on to a minute bikini pantie, but she liked to think that everything that went out of the shop had her own personal touch.

The nightgown was a special order for a trousseau, and she had enjoyed designing it and making it herself. But today she was unable to concentrate properly. The even pleating of the lace seemed tedious instead of absorbing, and every now and then she dropped her hands into her lap to stare into space.

Lunch time crawled round, and although she didn't feel like eating she made herself a sandwich and a cup of tea. She turned on the television, but the daytime soap operas with their unlimited characters and interminable problems merely bored and confused her, and she switched it off again.

Gritting her teeth, she finished sewing the lace, and thankfully put aside the nightgown. She took out a sketch book, and a couple of books of samples, and flipped through them. There were some small-check gingham in blue, red and mint green, and some narrow white ribbon lace. She thought they looked good together, and it would make a change from silks and lawns and nylons.

Her pencil stroked over the page, at first hesitantly, then with increasing vigour and sureness. She discarded one page, screwing it up to throw it on the floor, then began over again. Her concentration returned, pushing out the milling thoughts that had bothered her all morning. For a time she forgot about Drew and what had happened yesterday.

When she had finished, she looked at the paper critically, then looked again, her mouth forming a silent, 'Oh, no!'

The sketch was of a Victorian-style nightgown with puffed, frilled and lace-edged sleeves, and a tucked bodice decorated with lace, worn by a pert little girl with partially defined features and long hair under a frilled mob cap. She was holding a Wee-Willie-Winkie candlestick, and bare toes peeked from under the tucked hem of the gown.

Her pencil hovered, sketching in facial details, dark eyes, straight brows that gave the child a serious, winsome look, the faintest hint of a dimple in one cheek. Biting her lip so hard that it hurt, she scrawled, 'Holly' across the corner of the picture, then flung the book on the floor, and turned her face to the cushions and began to sob unrestrainedly.

When Gretta let herself in later, she found Karen asleep on the sofa, her face lightly flushed. She opened her eyes as Gretta picked up the sketch book and straightened the page, looking at the drawing.

Gretta looked up. 'I didn't mean to wake you.'

'You didn't. I must have been asleep for hours. What's the time?'

'About half-past five. I love this, Karen. Are you going in for a new line? You're going to do it in the gingham, are you? Wouldn't the red and white look great? 'Holly'—is that what you're going to call it? What a super idea. Should sell like hot cakes, specially before Christmas.'

'No!' Karen said sharply, reaching out for the sketch book as she struggled to sit up. 'I was just doodling . . . give it to me, I'll throw it away.'

Gretta looked horrified. 'You can't do that! I told you, it's great! Honestly, Karen. We've had quite a few enquiries about children's stuff——'

'I don't do children's clothes. You know that. They can get them at the children's specialist shops.'

'Why not try just this one design, and see how it goes?'

'No, Gretta. I don't want to sell for kids. It doesn't interest me.'

'Don't you like kids?' Gretta asked uncertainly.

Pain was squeezing her chest. Steadily, she said, 'I don't dislike them, I just ... I haven't had much to do with them. And I don't want to diversify my stock. The boutique's doing very well at the moment. Let's stick to what we know will sell.'

Gretta shrugged. 'You're the boss. Seems a pity though. And don't throw that away. It's too nice for that.'

Karen tried to smile as she thrust the book back into the drawer. 'How was your day? Busy?'

'Not bad. I sold that coffee lace petticoat. And your Mr Bridger called into the shop to ask how you were. He *is* like his voice, by the way. I told him I'd found you fast asleep last night, and this morning you'd had a hearty breakfast—well, you had breakfast, anyway—and that I'd let him know how you are now.'

'No, don't!' Karen said involuntarily.

Surprised, Gretta said, 'Why not? He's awfully concerned. I think he'd be round here himself, only he doesn't want you walking to the door to let him in. Anyway, I promised I'd ring him.'

'All right,' Karen said, rather tight-lipped. She certainly didn't want Drew coming himself to check on her progress, and she doubted that he cared that much. Perhaps he wanted to know if she was well enough to answer his questions. 'Phone him and tell him I'm feeling fine, the ankle's much better and I'll be back at work within a few days. Then don't phone him again. And he doesn't need to concern himself any more.'

'OK.' Gretta looked puzzled, but decided to keep her own counsel. 'Now, what do you want for tea?'

Two days later Karen was back at the boutique, limping slightly, and at Gretta's insistence spending most of her time sitting with her foot propped on a stool in the small back workroom screened from the public by a bead curtain. Here at least the phone was within reach, and she could contact her suppliers and do some bookwork.

The phone rang at ten o'clock while Gretta was busy serving a customer. Holding a pencil in one hand and still running it down a column of figures, Karen picked up the receiver and said, 'Lavender and Lace, can I help you?'

'How is ... *Karen*?' Drew's voice said.

As if she had been burnt, Karen dropped the receiver back on its cradle. She stared at the phone until it began to ring again insistently. It rang five times before she picked it up again, waving away Gretta who had appeared in the doorway, looking perplexed.

'Hello?' she said into the mouthpiece.

'That was pretty silly, wasn't it?' He sounded decidedly irritated.

'You took me by surprise. It was a reflex action.'

'What are you doing back at work?'

'Working.'

'Are you fit enough for that?'

'Yes. Thank you for asking. Now, I have customers waiting——'

'At a guess, I'd say that's a lie. But I get the message. I want to see you——'

'No.'

He paused. 'We have to talk, Karen. Surely you can see that?'

'No. If we hadn't accidentally bumped into each other the question wouldn't arise. There's nothing we need to talk about ... and I don't——'

'What about Holly?' he interrupted.

Her breath stopped in her throat. It was two seconds before she could say anything, and her lips would scarcely move as she finally asked, '*What* about her?'

'You want to know about her, don't you?'

Karen closed her eyes tightly, thankful that he couldn't see her face. The hand holding the telephone receiver was clammy. She swallowed, willing her voice to stay steady and uncaring. 'Not specially,' she lied. 'It's been a long time . . . she was only a . . .' but her lips refused to form the word 'baby'. 'To tell you the truth,' she added with great casualness, 'I can scarcely remember her.'

For a moment he was silent, and she thought she had disconcerted him. About to give him a cool goodbye, she stopped when he said flatly, 'You asked after her the other day.'

She recalled standing in front of him at the park, the words that he had wrenched from her, and the brutal taunt of his answer. Taking a firmer hold on the slippery plastic in her hand, she said, 'It . . . seemed to be expected.'

Again he didn't answer immediately. Then he said, 'I gave up expecting anything of you, Karen, a long time ago.'

She touched her tongue to dry lips. This time she couldn't hide the tremor in her voice. 'Yes, well, let's leave it at that, shall we?'

In a gritty voice he said, 'Wouldn't you like to see her?'

The suggestion threw her totally off balance. She felt as though she had been hit in the midriff with a heavy object. Her mouth opened in a soundless cry, and she gripped the receiver with both hands as though it was necessary to hold it steady. *Of course* she would like to see Holly. Often, she had woven elaborate fantasies, planned complicated disguises, pored over bus and train time-tables, and later, when she could have afforded to fly, plane schedules as well. Once, when Holly would have been five, she had bought tickets and got as far as the Cook Strait ferry. She had stood on the wharf and fought a savage inward battle with herself, arguing that no one would know her, remember her, and that if she stood at the school gates ... and knowing that in such a small place, someone would recognise her, someone would tell Drew, perhaps even talk to Holly, ask her questions that would puzzle and upset a small child ... and finally had watched the ferry sail without her while she stood in a bleak, heartless Wellington wind that dried the tears on her cheeks as they fell.

'*No,*' she said, the sound close to a moan of anguish. She gritted her teeth and tried again. 'No. I don't think that would be a good idea.'

'For you?' Bitterness laced his voice.

'For ... anyone. Surely you can see that ...'

A clean break, she had decided, after years of fighting the urge to give in, and many a visit to a doctor who had at first prescribed medication and finally told her bluntly that sleeping pills were not the answer to her problem. 'You obviously are under prolonged emotional stress. Try to cut loose from whatever it is that's causing that ... otherwise, I must warn you, you'll be running the risk of a complete mental breakdown.' She knew he was right, and if that happened, would someone contact Drew, bring her back into his life, while she, mentally incompetent, was powerless to prevent it? The complications would be horrendous. With a tremendous effort she managed to make herself regard the past as a closed chapter. To stop even thinking about resurrecting it.

'Holly needn't know,' Drew said. 'I wouldn't tell her who you are.' She knew he was angry, though he was trying to keep all emotion out of his voice. And if he was still angry with her, why this strange generosity?

Just once, she thought. Just one time. But she knew it would never be enough. And afterwards ... would she have to start forgetting all over again? *Forgetting?* An inner voice mocked her. *When have you ever forgotten?*

All along she had known, when she studied those
timetables week after week until her eyes hurt, when she
took that nightmare journey that she had never
completed, and later when she had hired a private
detective to gather information and then changed her
mind and paid him off because whatever he told her it
wouldn't be enough, that if she ever saw Holly again, it
wouldn't stop there. That there was no way she could
gather crumbs and not want the whole loaf. She would
be tempted to lie to herself, make up little deceitful,
treacherous excuses, tell herself that this time it would
be different, that things had changed, that everything
would be all right; and once she allowed herself within
the orbit of temptation, she didn't think she could resist
it. And there had always been the certainty, deep down,
that it was all impossible now, that in the intervening
years, Drew would have come to hate her . . .

'Well?' Drew was asking in her ear.

'No,' she said, suddenly acutely fearful. Why was he
doing this? She didn't trust him. He hadn't forgiven
her, she knew that. Even his kindness had an edge to it,
the resentment and anger inside breaking through the
thin shell of his control. Drew would never physically
attack a woman, but emotional barbs were something
else. She didn't know what his motive was in offering to
let her see Holly, but she was certain it was manipulative
rather than charitable. He wanted answers, reasons, and
those she couldn't bear to give him. The only safe course
was to refuse to have anything to do with him.
Gathering all her strength, thankful that he couldn't see
her white, strained face and the agony in her eyes, she
said, 'I don't want to see her. And I don't want to see
you, either. Please, Drew, just leave me alone.'

When she got home there was a florist's box on the
doorstep. She knew who it was from as soon as she saw

the long-stemmed, pale gold roses. But she put them on the kitchen table and left them there while she made herself scrambled eggs and toast, and set the plate on the table. It wasn't until she had drunk a cup of coffee and washed up that she finally opened the cellophane wrapper and lifted the lid to find the card. There was no message, just his name. She contemplated doing something dramatic like throwing the whole lot in the dustbin, but it wasn't the fault of the flowers, which were actually flawless, and it seemed a pity to take her feelings out on them. She found a vase and put them on the coffee table in the lounge. They would have looked good in the bedroom with its cream and amber décor, and she was sure he had known that when he chose them, but she couldn't have stood having them in there.

After three weeks she hadn't heard from Drew again, and she began to think that the roses had been a farewell, a tacit admission that he had given up and taken her advice to let go. Perhaps, after the initial impact of meeting her again had worn off, he had realised that nothing would be gained by re-opening old wounds. The tension that had held her in thrall began to relax.

Then late one Friday afternoon, while she was wrapping a purchase for a customer, and Gretta was keeping an eye on a couple of giggling teenagers who were trying everything on but fairly obviously had no intention of buying, she looked up and saw Drew entering the shop, and by his side was a girl of about ten or eleven years old ...

Shock held her rigid, and she felt the blood draining out of her face, leaving her forehead cold and moist.

His eyes found her, and briefly met her stunned gaze before Holly—it must be Holly, it couldn't be anyone else—tugged at his hand and urged him over to a far corner where a display mannequin stood wearing an outfit in black and red that was based on the saloon-girl style of the American Old West.

She heard Holly's light, excited voice without distinguishing the words, and Drew saying in amused tones, 'Yes, very glamorous, but not quite what we're looking for.'

Her customer said something, and she wrenched away her eyes, looking at the woman blankly, one hand holding the paper wrapping and the other apparently frozen to the tape dispenser.

The woman looked over her shoulder to glance at the newcomers, and returning her gaze to Karen said curiously, 'Are you all right?'

Karen pulled herself together. 'Yes, of course. I'm sorry. We don't often see a man in here.'

It wasn't exactly true. Quite a number of men came to buy pretty things for wives or girlfriends, and some even accompanied them when they shopped for themselves. But the woman said, 'No, I suppose not,' and smiled and nodded as Karen handed her the parcel.

Drew and Holly were examining a rack of matching slips and panties now, and another woman had wandered in and buttonholed Gretta, who was showing her their new range of bed jackets. The teenagers brought the things they had been trying on over to the counter, where they dropped them in a heap, saying, 'Nah, nothing fits, sorry,' and wandered out, jostling each other with much stifled laughter in the doorway. Karen picked up the crumpled garments and began to restore them carefully to their hangers.

'I don't think there's anything here for little girls,' she heard Drew say.

'Daddy!' Holly answered in a long-suffering voice. 'I'm going to be *eleven*!'

She could hear the smile in his reply. 'I know, chicken. But these are for grown-up women. Not—teenagers.

They're just not your size.'

'I'll ask,' Holly said.

Karen's stomach tied itself in a knot, knowing the child was approaching. Her hands clenched on a satin kimono, creasing the delicate cloth. It was too late to retreat, and Gretta was offering assistance to an elderly woman who had just come in and was looking about in a vaguely helpless way.

'Excuse me ...'

She forced herself to look up, longing and dread making a fierce, sickening mix inside her. She tried to smile, but all her energy was going into memorising the small face before her, the clear brown eyes under finely arched brows, the straight little nose, the long hair tied in a ponytail that emphasised the purity of the smooth, wide brow and childish profile.

'... do you have anything in my size?'

Somehow she unglued her tongue from the roof of her mouth. There was a standard answer, she had given it hundreds of times. 'I'm sorry, we only stock adult sizes. Try the children's boutique round the corner in the main street.'

Holly looked disgusted. 'We've been there.' She began to turn away.

With a sudden need to keep her talking, Karen said, 'Didn't you like anything they had?'

Making a face, Holly said, 'Oh, it's all right for little kids. *I* don't want Donald Duck on my nightie, thank you.'

'I suppose not,' Karen said foolishly, watching the play of expression over the girl's face, thinking how pretty she was, and how poised for a child of ten ... nearly eleven. 'Is it a nightie you're looking for?' she asked.

'Mm, I think so. It's my birthday next week, and Daddy says I'm old enough now for a nightie instead of pyjamas. He wouldn't let me have one before in case it caught on fire. But I want to pick it myself.' She smiled suddenly, and Karen thought painfully, *I was right about the dimple. It is still there.* And one of her teeth was a fraction crooked, there hadn't been quite enough room for it to grow. 'I mean, I didn't want a wincey job from Woollies. Not for a birthday!'

'No, of course not.' Karen's voice sounded strange to her, strangled in her throat.

Drew came up behind the child and put his hands on her shoulders. 'My daughter has her own ideas,' he said. 'Hello.'

He sounded so casual, but when she looked at him she saw in his eyes a watchfulness, a guarded expectancy. They hadn't wandered in here by accident. He had planned it for reasons of his own. Suddenly she felt furiously angry with him. How could he? How could he do that to her . . . to Holly? He wanted something of her, she didn't have any idea what. But using the child like this was unforgivable.

She nodded without speaking, wishing they would go, but Holly was saying wistfully, 'I thought when we came in here, we'd be sure to find something. Everything's so pretty.'

'And fairly pricey,' Drew said drily.

'Most of it has quite a lot of handwork included in the finishing. And nothing is mass produced,' Karen said. She had explained this before to customers who thought her prices a bit steep.

Holly looked up at him. 'You said you didn't mind splashing out a bit. Are they too dear?'

He smiled down at her. 'It's OK, I guess. You're not extravagant very often.'

'I'm not allowed to be, am I?' she said, grinning, and he tweaked her nose gently.

Turning back to Karen, Holly said, 'Are you *sure* you

don't have anything that *might* fit me? Even something just a teeny bit too big? I'm still growing.'

Knowing that she hadn't, Karen looked at the wide, pleading eyes and said, weakly, 'Well, what sort of thing did you have in mind?'

'Oh, something like this!' Holly danced across the shop and pulled from one of the racks a red gown with white trimmings and scarlet ribbons. 'Or this one!' She displayed a white broderie nightgown lavishly tucked and with ruched sleeves. 'Or that red and white spotted one's not bad.' She nodded toward another Victorian-style gown that was pinned to the wall above their heads. 'But they're all miles too big.'

'Yes, I'm afraid they are,' Karen agreed. 'There really isn't anything like that in a smaller size than an adult ten, and—I'm afraid you're not very big, are you?'

Holly grimaced disconsolately. 'I s'pose not.'

'I expect you'll find something nice in some other shop.'

'Mm. I guess. But nobody's got such *nice* things as you have.'

'Well, thank you.' Warmed by the praise, Karen was betrayed into rashness. 'Do you like gingham?'

'That square stuff, like curtains?'

'Well, yes. It used to be used for curtains a lot. But it makes rather nice nighties, too.'

'Does it?' She seemed a bit doubtful.

'Well, I think so. I was thinking . . .'

My God, she said to herself. *What am I doing? This is crazy.* But Holly was looking at her expectantly.

Drew said politely, 'Yes?'

She threw him a look of panic, almost suspecting him of using some form of mind control. Where had the idea come from, anyway? It had formed itself into words before she had even properly accepted it into her brain. Before she'd had time to think about it.

'I could make you a nightie,' she said, feeling drawn by fate, 'in time for your birthday. One designed for you, that would fit.'

'Oh, *could* you?' The pleased surprise on the child's face was enough to more than make up for the sardonic twist of her father's mouth, and the uneasy sensation Karen had that it hid some kind of triumph.

'What would that cost?' he enquired.

Holly's excitement dimmed, and in that moment Karen hated him. He wasn't short of cash, for heaven's sake, she thought angrily. He had a damned good job that obviously paid a pretty high salary. Why all the penny-pinching? Was he bringing Holly up to think he was poor?

'I suppose that would be very expensive,' Holly was saying doubtfully.

She said, 'No, not really. I hope you don't mind, but you'd be a sort of guinea pig. I haven't designed for young people before, and I'd like to try out this new idea that I have. If you like yours, I may make up some similar designs to sell to the public.' Lies, she thought, all lies.

'Daddy?'

Drew smiled down at his daughter's hopeful face. 'Sounds fine to me.'

She hugged his arm. 'Thank you, Daddy!'

'If you don't like it,' Karen said, 'there's no obligation, of course.' She was talking to Drew, really, but Holly said fervently. 'Oh, I'm *sure* I'll like it. I like every single thing in the shop!'

'You said you hated the black leather-look one with the garter,' her father reminded her.

'Well, *nearly* everything! Anyway, aren't you lucky I didn't like it! You'd never let me have anything like that, and I would have sulked for days!' She giggled at him, and he grinned back and playfully slapped her small behind. 'That'll be enough, young lady.'

'Do you want a price now?' Karen asked him, suddenly businesslike.

'No. I'm sure you'll put the right price on it,' he said smoothly. His eyes challenged her, and she deliberately kept her face schooled to express nothing but courteous attention to the customer. 'When will it be ready?'

She glanced at the calendar on the wall behind the counter. 'This is the fourteenth. What day is her birthday?'

The faint smile that had still lingered on his lips vanished as his teeth snapped together. She felt a mild, mean satisfaction. Their eyes clashed, his murderous, and hers, with an effort of will, merely enquiring.

Holly said, 'Wednesday the nineteenth. Is that enough time?'

'Plenty.' Usually she allowed two to three weeks for a special order, but this would be finished if she had to delay everyone else's and work all night to do it. To Drew she said, 'You could pick it up on Tuesday.'

'Thank you.' He seemed barely able to bring himself to say it.

She said, 'I'll just take your measurements, Holly. Would you like to come into the workroom for a moment?'

She still had the straight-up-and-down figure of a child, Karen thought as she jotted down the statistics after using her tape measure. But there was a slight hint already of budding breasts. It wouldn't be very long before the child became a young woman. A faint ache tugged at her within her own breast, and she said briskly, 'You can put your jacket back on, now, Holly. That's all I need.'

'How did you know my name?'

The question jolted her. Stupid, how stupid of me . . . What on earth was Drew playing at? Didn't he realise that something like this might happen? Was it what he *wanted*?

But there was a simple way out. 'I ... heard your father say it.'

'Did you?' She looked puzzled. Surely she wouldn't remember, couldn't be sure, that Drew hadn't used her name since they came into the shop?

'Come on,' Karen said. 'He's waiting for you.'

They went out through the bead curtain. Gretta had dealt with the other customer and was talking to Drew.

He turned and smiled at Holly. 'All set?'

'Yes.' She looked up at Karen. 'Thank you very much.'

'Let's go, then,' Drew said, his hand on Holly's hair. He nodded to Karen and said goodnight to Gretta, who smiled back at him with all her gypsy charm as she answered, 'Goodnight, Mr Bridger.'

Let *him* explain that one away, Karen thought. No doubt he would, to Holly's satisfaction.

To Gretta she said, 'It's ten to six. Let's close up early and go home.'

CHAPTER THREE

KAREN worked over the weekend on the nightgown for Holly and its matching mob cap. By Monday morning they were wrapped in tissue and packed in a box with the boutique's name and trademark on the lid, a tiny lavender sachet tied in with the satin ribbon that bound it, and a deckle-edged plain card attached to the bow. She slipped it on to the shelf under the counter and wondered if she could make some excuse not to come in the next day. She should have told Drew it wouldn't be ready before late afternoon, and found a pretext to leave early. But she hadn't thought quickly enough, and it wouldn't be fair to leave Gretta to cope on her own all day.

He was most likely to come at lunchtime, she thought. She usually took her lunch break between one and two. The day she had bumped into Drew, she had thought a proper lunch and a change of scene would help cure her headache, but often she would go out for a sandwich or a pie and bring it back to eat in the workroom so that she was on call if the shop was busy. Tuesday was normally fairly quiet, and she said to Gretta that morning, 'Do you mind if I go out for lunch today?'

'I don't mind. Are you having it with Mr Bridger?'

Startled, Karen said, 'No! What makes you think that?'

Gretta shrugged, 'Well, you did before, didn't you? And he's coming in today, isn't he?'

'Actually, I didn't have lunch with him,' Karen said, turning to adjust a garment on one of the display models. 'He just happened to be there when I fell.'

'You mean you'd never met him before?'

'I didn't say that. We ... hadn't seen each other for

41

years, and I'd been talking to him. I tripped as I was walking away.'

'Oh.' Gretta looked thoughtful. 'He's married, I suppose?'

Karen was glad she had her back to her assistant. Very levelly, she said, 'A man with a daughter is presumably married. I told you, I haven't seen him for years. Pass me that tin of pins, will you? This has lost one. And could you go and open up the parcel that came from the warehouse yesterday? I think it might be the order of aqua nylon that I've been waiting for.'

Drew must have taken an early lunch. She had sent Gretta off for hers, and was watching the clock when he walked in at barely five past twelve. There was no one in the shop, and he came straight to where she stood behind the counter, putting price tickets on a pile of lacy briefs. In these surroundings, the acme of femininity, his masculine presence seemed intensified, a dangerous intrusion. Already she could feel the tension humming between them. She steadied herself against the counter, trying to hide her acute awareness of him.

He said, 'Hello, Karen,' at the same moment that she gave him a cool professional smile and said, 'Good afternoon. Your parcel is ready.'

She bent and brought out the box, placing it on the counter, and handing him the envelope that had been lying on the lid. 'And this is your invoice. I hope it's satisfactory.'

She had been tempted to bill him for some astronomical sum, but resisted the urge for Holly's sake, and the price was extremely moderate, as she had promised. He opened the envelope, glanced at the slip of paper inside and took a credit card out of his pocket. 'This is all right?'

'Yes, certainly.' She took the card company's form from a drawer and said, 'Would you like to see the gown?'

'I'm sure it's fine. And I'd hate to disturb the wrapping. You've gone to a lot of trouble.'

'Not at all,' she said coolly. 'It's our standard gift-wrap.' It was actually quite easy to open—just a matter of a piece of tape holding the ends of the ribbon on the bottom.

She filled in the credit form and handed it to him for his signature, noting the handsome silver pen that he used. As she tore off his copy, he pulled the gift box towards him and wrote on the card she had provided for Holly's present.

Karen handed over the folded slip, and he took it in his left hand, holding out the pen to her. 'Perhaps you'd like to add something?' he suggested, indicating the gift card.

Her breath caught in her throat, hurtfully. 'I don't think that would be appropriate,' she said, her voice not quite steady.

'Don't you?' He paused, and she felt his eyes on her bent head as she busied her shaking hands, putting away the other copies of his credit invoice. 'Well . . . perhaps you're right,' he said.

Go away, she cried silently, her heart thumping uncomfortably. *Why are you doing this to me?* It could only be from a desire to hurt, and although one part of her accepted that he must feel justified, she was no masochist, and she was determined not to let him know how easily he was succeeding.

'These look . . . enticing.' He picked up a triangular wisp of white lace and satin from the counter, and examined it with interest, then dropped it and lifted a red heart-shaped one, and then a minute black one with ruched satin ribbons holding the two scraps of cloth together.

Resisting an urge to tear them out of his hands, she said, 'They're not suitable for little girls.'

His eyebrows rose. In apparent amusement, he said, 'I agree. I wasn't—actually—thinking of a *little* girl.' He picked over the small heap of frills and nonsense again, and said, 'I'll have this . . . and this.' He had chosen the red hearts and a black bikini-style covered with rows of narrow lace frills.

For a moment she was breathless, torn by an absurd need to scream, *Who for?* She clamped her teeth together tightly and swallowed, then removed the price tags she had just put on, and folded the garments inside each other. 'Will there be anything else?'

'Yes.' His voice sounded clipped, and she glanced up. His eyes held a hard mockery. 'I'd like to buy a nightgown . . . something glamorous . . . the kind of thing I couldn't very well buy with my daughter around, if you know what I mean?'

'Yes,' she said, her mouth drying. 'I know what you mean.' She hoped he saw nothing but contempt in her eyes as she raised them again to his. 'I'm sure you'll find something if you look around.'

His shrug and smile were a parody of self-deprecation. 'Would you help me? You know how we men are at this sort of shopping . . . and you must know what you have here.'

She would have done it for another customer without a thought, and she was desperately trying to treat him like any other customer. Her lips stiff, she said, 'Of course. What size?'

As she came round the counter, he ran his eyes over her with brutal frankness, making no pretence that it was meant to be other than an insult, a mental assault, but his voice was bland as he said, 'Oh, about your size, I think. Perhaps just a shade less . . . slim.'

Why didn't he say skinny and be done with it? she thought angrily. 'Probably a twelve,' she said. She knew from experience that men usually tended to overestimate size. 'They're over here.' She led the way to the rack and said crisply, 'Do you have any preference as to colour?'

He shrugged. 'Not particularly. Perhaps not white, though.'

Of course not white, she thought with grim cynicism. She took from the rack a transparent, black nylon shortie, the lace-edged front held together by half a dozen metallic gold bows, with its own matching panties and a frilled garter decorated with a tiny gold bell that tinkled lightly. It was undeniably sexy, bordering on the vulgar, and she saw Drew's lips twitch slightly as his brows went up and he said, 'A bit obvious, don't you think?'

'I thought it might suit your taste.'

He threw her an inimical look and said, 'Do you have something more ... sophisticated?'

Two women wandered into the shop, and she said, 'Excuse me, please,' thankfully approaching the new customers with a polite, 'Can I help you?'

'Just looking, thank you,' one of them said firmly, obviously not wanting help, and Karen returned, defeated, to Drew's side.

He had taken out a dusky pink two-piece set that she had based on the clinging bias-cut gowns and see-through feather-trimmed négligés of the thirties' movie queens.

'I like this,' he said. 'But it's difficult to picture it ... Perhaps if you could hold it up against you for a minute, I could see what it looks like?'

He gave her a hopeful, enquiring look of masculine helplessness, completely spurious, and held out the hanger to her, giving a glance over her shoulder to the two women who were now riffling through the next rack.

Inwardly raging, she took the hanger and held it against her, while he stood back with a judicious air, taking his time.

'Maybe ...' he said doubtfully. 'What else do you have?'

Silently she replaced the hanger and pulled out a pair

of black satin embroidered pyjamas.

'No,' he said, shaking his head. 'Not pyjamas. Try this one, would you?' He handed her a pink lace shift, then a black and red chorus-girl copy like the one Holly had admired, and inspected them both as she obediently stood before him, seething all the time. Then he said, 'What about this?'

The long dark-gold satin gown had a deep cross-over neckline and high waist, and an unusual tulip-petal skirt that repeated the cross-over design of the bodice. It was one of her favourites, depending on cut and material rather than trimming for its attraction.

'I like this,' he said. 'It's awfully hard to tell, though . . . I don't suppose you'd try it on for me . . . properly?'

Karen had had enough. 'I'm not your model!' she snapped. 'Try it on yourself!'

She saw the startled looks of the two women before they hurried out of the shop, and as Drew looked after them, grinning, she had a strong desire to hit him.

'I don't think it would suit me, somehow,' he said, with laughter in his voice.

'It might be funny to you,' she said furiously, 'but you've just lost me a possible sale. This place is my livelihood.'

'I didn't do a thing,' he said. 'You lost your temper, darling, and scared them off. If you yell at the customers, what can you expect?'

'You were deliberately baiting me!'

'Haven't you had awkward customers before? Surely you've learned how to deal with them?'

'Yes. I usually give *perverts* short shrift.'

He pursed his lips. 'Nasty, darling. And untrue.'

'Is it?' She glared at him.

He laughed a little. 'At least you've stopped your plastic mannequin act. You're giving a fair imitation of a human being now, if a bad-tempered one.'

Suddenly realising that it was just what he had been aiming at, she bit her tongue on the retort she had been about to make. She had annoyed him by keeping her cool, and he had needled her until she lost it. She wished she hadn't fallen into the trap so easily.

Gretta swung in through the doorway, giving Drew a wide smile. 'Hello, Mr Bridger.' She cast him a sidelong glance as she made for the back room, and said, 'I won't be a minute, Karen, if you want to go to lunch now.'

It was nearly one, Karen realised. She turned to Drew, and said with great calm, 'Will that be all, then?'

She expected him to say yes, and pay the few dollars for the panties he had bought. But he took down the gold gown again and said, 'I'll take this.'

A hollow feeling in her stomach, she took the garment from him and returned to the counter. As he followed, she read out the price tag to him. It was far too much to pay just to make a point, but he didn't move an eyelash. So he hadn't just been pretending in order to annoy her. 'Do you want them all wrapped together?' she asked.

He placed the plastic card in front of her again as she unfolded tissue and plain mauve paper. 'Yes, please,' he said. 'Aren't you going to gift-wrap them?'

Sheer outrage possessed her for a moment, but she managed to say levelly, 'If you like. I didn't realise . . .'

Amused, he said, 'Well, they certainly aren't for me.'

She fished out a box from under the counter and quickly packed the things, completing the docket in stoic silence. 'Don't you want to write on the card?' she asked him as he tucked the pen back into his pocket.

'Later,' he said. 'This one's rather private.'

I'll bet, she thought viciously. Aloud, she said, 'Be careful you don't muddle the boxes,' and gave him a wholly artifical smile.

'I won't.'

He picked them up as Gretta sauntered out, the bead curtains clashing faintly behind her. 'Buying something nice for your wife, Mr Bridger?' she asked innocently.

There was scarcely a moment's pause before he said, 'Yes.' He smiled at her, and his nod in Karen's direction was a masterpiece of indifference. 'Thanks a lot.'

'There,' Gretta said as she lounged on the counter, gazing after him. 'He is married.'

Rather sharply, Karen said, 'You know perfectly well that not every man who says he's buying for his wife is bound to be telling the truth.'

Gretta's aristocratic nose wrinkled in thought. 'Yeah. But he doesn't strike me as one of that sort.'

'Anyway, you already knew he was married.'

'Not necessarily. Could be divorced or widowed or something. Men with wives don't usually go shopping with their daughters, do they? Specially for things like undies.'

No, they didn't. And, Karen realised, she had been unconsciously assuming that because he did, Drew didn't have a wife. But he could have remarried. It certainly wasn't impossible. There was absolutely no reason why he shouldn't have, and several very cogent ones for him to have done so.

Supposing he had, and supposing that the nightgown and the daring briefs had been for his wife? But somehow she couldn't make herself believe it.

On Friday night just before the shop closed, he came in again with Holly.

'She wanted to thank you personally,' he told Karen.

Holly smiled at her and said, 'It's lovely. And it fits like a dream. Thank you very much.'

'That's quite all right. It's our business to keep clients happy.' She caught Drew's quick frown of censure, and added, 'I'm glad you like it.'

'Daddy said you must have had to hurry to do it in time for my birthday. It was awfully nice of you.'

'It really didn't take very long.'

'Well, thanks anyway.' The child shifted on her feet, slightly less self-possessed than usual, and then tugged at her father's sleeve, and tiptoed to whisper in his ear as he bent towards her.

He straightened and looked at Karen. 'I promised Holly I'd take her to a café for supper. We'd like you to join us.'

'It's very kind of you, but——'

'Please,' Holly said tensely, her face slightly flushed with suspense. 'It's a sort of thank you.'

'You've already thanked me very nicely,' Karen said weakly. 'And your father has p——'

She didn't dare complete the sentence, meeting the dark blaze in Drew's eyes. If she mentioned that her services had been bought and paid for, he looked as if he might kill her. It was true, and she shouldn't have hesitated, but Holly's bright, anticipatory gaze stopped her. And the enticement of spending half an hour with her. That, of course, was what made her hesitate, torn between overwhelming longing and deadly caution.

And caution didn't stand a chance against a child's brown eyes. 'Thank you,' she said, not looking at Drew. 'That would be very nice.'

Holly smiled brilliantly. 'Goody! Where would you like to go?'

'Anywhere you say. Let me lock up first, and I'll meet you outside.'

Gretta was serving a customer, and Karen waited while the woman paid and left. 'Shall I shut the door?' she asked, casting a curious glance at Drew and Holly, who were loitering in the arcade, looking at the window display.

'Yes.' Karen opened the cash register and began scooping out the money. 'You go. I'll cash up and get this into the safe.'

'Are you sure?' Usually they made it a rule that they both stayed until the day's takings were safely stowed away.

'Yes, it'll only take a few minutes. Your boyfriend will be waiting.' Gretta had produced a speedy succession of boyfriends in the eighteen months that she had worked at the boutique, some of such alarming appearance that

Karen, mindful of the boutique's image, had tactfully asked her assistant to ensure that they waited for her at a discreet distance.

'Yeah, he is. Well, if you're sure you're OK. Is that Mr Bridger waiting for *you*?'

Karen flushed. 'Yes. Holly—the little girl—asked me to have supper with them.'

'Oh, did she? Bet her dad put her up to it.'

'I don't think so.'

Gretta stared. 'You can't be that innocent. Not at your age. If I were you, I'd find out for sure if he's married or not. Anyway, he's big enough to put off any robbers that might be lurking round the corner, so you'll be OK. See you Monday.'

Karen added up the cash and quickly scribbled down the total before placing the money in the small safe.

She looked in the mirror on the wall of the tiny washroom and renewed her lipstick, then picked up her bag and went through to the front of the shop, switching off lights as she went. The plate glass door slid shut and she locked it and placed the key in her bag, then turned to the man and the girl standing nearby and said, 'I'm ready.'

It was strange sitting opposite Drew at the small café table. Holly sat beside him, tucking into hamburger and chips, chocolate sundae and a thickshake, but both her father and Karen had opted for toasted sandwiches and cheesecake with coffee.

There was little conversation. Holly was fully occupied, Karen felt tongue-tied, and Drew didn't seem inclined to talk, though his watchful gaze was making Karen decidedly uncomfortable.

When she pushed away half of her cheesecake, he looked up at her sharply and said, 'Don't you want it?'

Karen shook her head, and Holly said, 'Can I have it?'

Karen smiled disbelievingly. Holly was half-way

through an enormous sundae. She started to say, 'If you want it ...'

But Drew was saying bluntly, 'No, you can't.'

Holly looked hurt and surprised. 'Why? I always eat what *you* don't want.'

'That's different.'

Holly frowned, working it out. 'Because you're my father?'

'Yes.'

'Oh.' She looked at Karen and said cheerfully, 'Sorry.'

'It's all right. You can have it, honestly.' Transferring her gaze to Drew, she asked drily, 'Do you starve her at home?'

'No, I feed her on bread and water, don't I, chicken?' He tweaked at Holly's hair, and she giggled and said, 'Yes, and he keeps me in this dark dungeon with spiders and rats and *slime*, and I'm only allowed out on Friday nights.'

'I'm sure.' Karen smiled at her, and Drew said, 'I knew I shouldn't let you watch the Sunday Horrors. What about that birthday party on Wednesday? Sausage rolls, chicken patties, and tons of potato crisps, not to mention that disgustingly sticky dessert and the birthday cake.'

'Oh, yes, he did let me out for that!' Holly said earnestly to Karen. Then she turned and rubbed her cheek against his sleeve, like a mischievous kitten. '*Thank* you, Daddy.'

'Brat,' he said, gently flicking her nose with a finger.

Watching them, Karen felt a sudden lump obstructing her throat.

Drew moved the cheesecake towards her and said, 'Why don't you eat it? It'll do you good.'

'Fatten me up, you mean?'

'You could do with a bit more weight.'

Holly said accusingly, 'It's not polite to make personal remarks.'

'She's right, you know,' Karen taunted him, enjoying siding with Holly. Suddenly she felt almost light-hearted, the child's infectious high spirits rubbing off on her.

Holly finished the ice cream and put the long spoon down. 'Are you Miss Lacey or Mrs Lacey?' she suddenly asked. 'On the shop window it just said, "Karena Lacey".'

'I'm ... just Karena. Karen to my friends.'

Holly wriggled, looking slightly dissatisfied. She glanced at her father and finally said, 'Can I call you Karen?'

Huskily, not looking at Drew, Karen said, 'Yes, of course you can.'

When she dared to glance at him again, he was staring grimly into his coffee cup.

Holly was discreetly sucking the bubbles from the bottom of her milkshake, and picking up the last lump of melting ice-cream with the plastic straw. Karen watched her bemusedly. She had forgotten how children were able to wallow in enjoyment.

'That was gorgeous!' Holly said, closing her eyes blissfully. Then turning to her father, she whispered, 'I need to go to the toilet.'

Drew looked about, then said, 'Over there.'

'Shall I come with you?' Karen offered.

The child looked surprised. 'No, thanks. It's all right.'

'She learned to be independent early,' Drew said as they watched her wend her way between the tables.

Karen just stopped herself from wincing. 'She seems very confident. Does she often issue invitations to ... to perfect strangers? Or did you put her up to it?'

'I had nothing to do with it. She's looking for a mother figure. That's why she was trying to find out if you're married.'

Her hands clenched themselves tightly in her lap. Did he have to twist the knife like this?

She said, 'What about the woman you bought the

nightgown for? I take it she's not a mother figure?'

He pushed away his coffee cup and leaned back in his chair, regarding her with an enigmatic look. 'Not exactly.'

'Aren't you ... are you married?'

'Again,' he said, after a moment, 'not exactly.'

'What does that mean?' she asked him, challengingly.

Suddenly he leaned forward, scowling, but keeping his voice low. 'What the *hell* kind of game are you playing? It means *yes*, of course I'm *married*. To *you*.'

Her hands were clammy fists. 'I thought ... you might have got a divorce.'

'No.'

'My lawyer did contact you?'

'Yes. Saying you wouldn't contest. I wasn't interested. All I wanted from him was your address, and he wouldn't give it to me.'

'If you change your mind,' she said jerkily, 'it's easier now. After two years' separation. You wouldn't even need to contact me to get a dissolution. I thought you might have done ...'

'Look, I know about the divorce laws, OK?' He suddenly sucked in his breath. '*You* didn't ...'

Karen shook her head. 'No. I would have told you.'

'Why did you never contact us?' he said starkly, suddenly, and she shrank back from him, turning her head away.

'Here's Holly,' she said with relief, and waited for the girl to resume her seat.

'We might as well leave.' Drew stood up. Karen was glad to follow suit, and Holly reluctantly wriggled out of her chair, complaining that she had only just sat down again.

'It's past your bedtime, brat,' Drew said firmly. 'Come on.'

Outside, he said to Karen, his voice so even that she knew he was curbing his temper, 'Can we drop you somewhere? Do you have a car?'

She shook her head. 'I'll get a bus. It's not far.'

'We'll take you home.' He took her arm, and when she tried to pull away, he said under his breath, 'Don't argue, Karen. I'm not in the mood for it.'

Rebellious but silent, she allowed him to take her to one of the city's multi-storeyed car-parks. Drew let Holly operate the elevator button for the right floor, and as they travelled upwards she turned to Karen and said, 'Next time I want to buy a present, I'll come to your shop.'

'You couldn't afford her prices,' Drew said.

'Oh, I s'pose not.' Holly grimaced. 'Oh, well, can I come and see you, anyway?'

Yes, oh yes please! her heart pleaded. But of course it wouldn't happen. It was a child's temporary fancy, and she would forget about it in a few days or weeks.

The lift stopped as Karen said unsteadily, 'Of course you can.'

Drew guided her to the car with a hard hand on her arm, and put her in the front beside him. Holly climbed into the back and, by the time they arrived at Karen's place, had dozed off in the corner. 'Say goodbye to her for me,' she said softly, getting out as quietly as she could.

He accompanied her to the door of the flat, and stood by while she put the key in the lock. Pushing it open, she said, 'Thank you for the supper, I enjoyed it.'

'Perhaps we should do it again some time.'

'I ... don't think so.'

'Holly would like it.' The knife twisted yet again.

She made an agitated move to go inside, but he put a hand on the door jamb, and the other held her arm, turning her to face him. 'Did you get my roses?'

'Yes,' she said, disconcerted. 'I'm sorry, I should have thanked you for them. They were beautiful.'

'I suppose they're dead now.'

'Yes, I'm afraid so.'

'Like a lot of other things,' he said, looking down at her averted face.

She didn't answer, and after a moment he said, 'Goodnight, Karen.'

The hand on her arm tightened, and his other arm came round her, and she found herself meeting his kiss as though she had been expecting it. Her mouth was soft and opened under his, even though there was lingering anger in the way his lips moved on hers, almost bruising them, and for seconds she stayed in his arms, the blood running hot and molten in her veins. For seconds, and then she pulled free, and only his hands on her arms held her as they stared at each other in the dim light from the distant street lamp, breathing hard.

'Well,' he said, 'maybe some things aren't so dead, after all.'

It shouldn't have happened, she told herself as she stood in the little entry-way, listening to the engine note of the car dying away. She shouldn't have let it happen. She went up the stairs without switching on any lights, knowing the familiar way in the dark. She wondered if he had planned it. An experiment to find out if she would respond to him again, perhaps to find out if he still enjoyed kissing her.

She should have refused the invitation, it was madness to have anything to do with him ... with Holly.

The bathroom light made her blink. She cleaned her teeth fiercely and washed her face with vigour, noticing that her eyes were bright and clear and the pupils enlarged, and her cheekbones, even when scrubbed clean of make-up, had a faint warm glow. She hadn't seen herself looking so vitally alive for years.

'It was only a kiss,' she muttered to her reflection. 'You fool!'

She pulled the pins from her hair, shaking out her hair impatiently, and was arrested by the reflection in the glass. She looked wantonly seductive, and for a moment her own image fascinated her. This was how she might look for *him* . . .

Deliberately, she made a face at herself. 'Narcissus.' She smoothed the fine hair back from her face and began to braid it quickly with nimble fingers as she made her way back to the bedroom. Tonight she would skip the brushing for once. She didn't want to be reminded . . .

But lying in bed, with a silk nightdress caressing her skin, and the warm darkness kissing her eyelids, she was hot and restless and unable to sleep. Images of the past crowded into her mind, her body was awakening to desires she had long suppressed. She buried her head in the pillow and tried to blot out all feeling, all thought, all memory. Later, she turned on the light, picked up a book and read thirty pages without understanding a word. It didn't help. Nothing helped. She didn't sleep until near dawn, and then she woke late with a fuzzy head and brief, snapshot memories of erotic dreams.

I was all right, she thought. I was doing all right. Why did he have to find me? I don't *want* this. Oh, please God, make him leave me alone.

CHAPTER FOUR

FOR a city with a population approaching a million, Auckland seemed a very small place. Several times over the years Karen had narrowly missed bumping into people she had once known, only her changed appearance and a glassy stare saving her on at least two occasions from recognition, and she supposed she was lucky that for so long she had avoided detection. Twice in the next week she caught a glimpse of Drew, once in the public library when she was changing her books, and once as she was hurrying down the broad, brick-paved slope of Vulcan Lane where a street theatre was entertaining an appreciative lunchtime crowd. Each time she hurried out of sight as quickly as she could, her heart pounding as though she was in some physical danger. Stupid, she knew, but she couldn't help the panic need to flee from any chance of meeting him again. She tried to tell herself that he wouldn't seek her out again, that the cruel experiment of the kiss signalled a final end to their relationship, but she knew it wasn't so. He would be back, and the hiatus was only a cat-and-mouse ploy to keep her on tenterhooks while he gathered his forces and planned his next move. Drew had never been a man to give up easily.

It was no surprise to see him waiting one evening as she locked up the boutique after work. She was carrying a couple of bolts of material, wrapped in brown paper, which she was taking home to cut out, and he moved over to her and said, 'Let me take that. I'll give you a lift home.'

'No thanks,' she said. 'I'm meeting someone.'

'Where?'

'Is that any of your business?'

57

'I'll carry your parcel and walk with you.'

'I'd hate to take you out of your way,' she said. 'Really, I'm quite capable of carrying my own parcels. I've been doing it for ten years.'

'And whose choice was that?' His inflexion was soft and deadly, and she flinched away from it. He said, 'Let's stop sparring, Karen. You're not meeting anyone, are you? And I'm not just offering you a lift out of the goodness of my heart and because I have time to kill. I've got to see you.'

'You've seen me several times lately. It hasn't done either of us much good, has it?'

'We can't talk with Holly around, and you know it.'

'Where is she now? With your mother?'

'My mother?' He seemed nonplussed. 'My mother died.'

'Shock washed over her. Her eyes dilated, staring at him. 'Died?'

'Soon after you left she had a heart attack, and from then on she was never well. She had another attack that killed her about six months later.'

'But I thought that she . . . I thought you would have . . . She wasn't old. Oh, Drew, I'm so sorry! I didn't know anything about it . . .'

His glance flicked over her coldly. 'No, well, you took good care not to, didn't you? Look, we can't talk here. Come on, let's go to my car.'

Still mentally reeling from the unexpected news, she allowed him to take the parcel from her arms and lead her to where his car was parked. He threw the materials on the back seat and said, 'Do you want to go home, or shall we find some neutral territory?'

'What do you mean?'

Impatiently he said, 'It's a bit early, but we could go somewhere for a couple of leisurely drinks, and then dinner.'

Neutral ground sounded like a good idea. A nice public bar and restaurant where a civilised discussion couldn't turn into something more physical, and social convention prohibited raised voices.

She said, 'All right, but I don't want to be out very late, I have some work to do.'

He seemed surprised at her acceptance, but quickly hid it and started the engine, asking, 'Any preferences?'

Karen shook her head. 'I'll leave it to you.'

'How remarkably amenable of you,' he murmured.

'If you're going to spend the time sniping at me, perhaps we should call the whole thing off right now,' she retorted.

He swung the car into the stream of traffic. 'I'll try not to. Only I'm afraid it's a little difficult to refrain when you're around.'

'Then I don't understand why you want to be around me.'

He glanced at her and said under his breath, 'Maybe you're not the only one.'

'What?' she asked, wondering if she had heard right.

'Never mind.' A bus thundered past them and nearly clipped the front bumper as it roared into the lane ahead of them, then came to a halt in front of a red light and sat panting and belching puffs of black smoke from its exhaust. Drew swore quietly, and she firmly closed her lips to allow him to concentrate on negotiating the rush-hour traffic.

At this time of the day, the city was noisy and reeked of petrol pollution, and the denizens of the offices and shops were anxious to shake its dust from their feet—or rather, from the tyres of their Skodas, Fords and Mitsubishis. But in the morning they would be back in their offices, glancing up now and then to look out at the sunshine dancing on the harbour, with the gently sloping hump of Rangitoto drowsing in the distance, perhaps to wish that they were aboard one of the yachts cavorting daintily about in seemingly aimless fashion between the island and the graceful bow of the Harbour Bridge. When she had first come to Auckland, Karen had been lonely and heartsick, and short of money. She had welcomed the low-paid job she managed to obtain in a clothing factory because it brought her a wage that provided the bare necessities of food, clothes and first a hostel bed and then a dingy one-room flat. She had been intimidated by the size, the speed and the impersonality of the city, but had wanted the camouflage of anonymity that it gave her.

She had been only going through the motions of living, enveloped in a shroud of depression that threatened to engulf her. After those first few years of simply gritting her teeth and forcing herself to work, eat, and at least make an attempt at sleep each day, spending her spare time locked in her spartan room giving in to her obsession with planning impossible reunions, she made a conscious decision to pull herself out of the slough and forge some kind of normal life for herself.

First she discovered the public library. Reading was something she had always enjoyed, and a good book had the power to make her forget herself and her painful memories for minutes at a time. She was to find that the span became gradually longer. Then she began taking long walks at the weekends, exploring the Domain gardens that surrounded the imposing, white, classical-style building of the War Memorial Museum, a favourite venue for family outings and tourist trips. Sometimes on a fine day, she would sit for hours watching a succession of children throwing bread scraps to the ducks on the pond, but that was morbid and eventually she stopped going there. She tried visiting some of the city's smaller parks, and the grassy slopes of the dormant volcanoes on which many of the older homes were built, and the waterfront drive which ran for miles around the bays and beaches. Always there were children, but she gradually hardened herself to their presence until she was able to ignore them.

Occasionally she treated herself to a bus ride to one of

the further suburbs, many of them fronting pleasant beaches which were a summertime paradise, or a ferry trip to the north shore of the harbour where more tree-shaded suburbs and more beaches awaited. Once she took a day trip to Rangitoto and climbed to the summit to eat her lunch overlooking the other islands that lay strewn on the Hauraki Gulf. And later, when she had left the factory for a better job in a high-class clothing shop, she explored the inner city and discovered the cluster of secondhand bookshops in High Street, the delicatessens and vegetarian food shops springing up nightly like mushrooms crammed into spaces between offices and department stores, and the boutiques that were producing overseas fashions within days of their appearing in shows in Paris, London, and New York. She spent numerous Saturday mornings in the multi-ethnic shopping centre of Ponsonby Road, and among the classy speciality merchants of Parnell Village and Remuera.

Tired of long, lonely evenings, she had enrolled in classes at night school, and taken courses in business management, design and technical drawing. Those had brought her not only new skills, but contact with other people, and she began to form relationships again, not close ones, but easy, non-demanding friendships, and the occasional date.

Brought up in a small town, she had found the metamorphosis to city dweller painful but rewarding. She was at home here now. She knew the places to get a taxi on Friday nights, the streets to avoid after dark, where to go to listen to good jazz or bad-to-brilliant poetry, which restaurants served the best, though not necessarily the most expensive, food, which series of buses would take the traveller to the furthest of the suburbs, and where to buy fresh bread or a good lunch on a Sunday. Now, of course, she could have afforded to buy a car, but she hadn't bothered. She could use public transport to go anywhere in the city, and she seldom wanted to leave it.

'Do you know this place?' Drew asked her, pulling up opposite a building with a striped awning outside and pot-plants on the window-sills.

'No, I don't.' She had a small circle of friends and a larger number of business acquaintances with whom she sometimes ate out, but this restaurant was new to her—not surprisingly, since restaurants in Auckland had proliferated lately, and many established ones passed from one proprietor to another so quickly that the local gourmet columnists complained of not being able to keep up with their changing fortunes.

'It was recommended to me,' Drew said. 'Shall we try it?'

The atmosphere seemed pleasant, with an unobtrusive décor featuring twenties prints on the wall, and lots of greenery. Karen freshened up in the ladies' room and joined Drew at the bar.

'Is it still gin and tonic?' he asked her.

Karen shook her head. 'I'll have a glass of white wine, please.'

They sat on a curved banquette at a small table, and Karen kept her eyes on her drink, even when she wasn't sipping at it. Drew pushed over a small dish of peanuts, but she shook her head. He picked up his glass and drank, and she covertly watched his hands, remembering the feel of them, the gentleness and strength of his long fingers. She swallowed, and looked away.

Putting down his glass, he said, 'How long have you had the boutique?'

'Nearly two years, now.'

'Where did you get the money?'

'I have a bank loan.'

'You'd still need to put in quite a bit yourself.'

She raised her eyes. 'That's right, I did.' She had saved all she could from her wages, starting with the factory job and then moving up to assistant and then manager of a Queen Street clothing store, and had started off in a small way, 'moonlighting' by making exquisite undies for friends of friends and selling to a few boutiques, before she had decided she was ready to open her own, specialising in her unique designs.

He turned his glass, looking down at it, then glanced up and said, 'Did you have help?'

'Not the kind you mean,' she said defiantly. 'It was all done with hard work and a certain amount of sacrifice.'

'And were Holly and I part of the sacrifice?'

She paled and pressed her lips together to stop them trembling. 'I hadn't thought of the boutique or anything like it, then.'

'I'd like to know what you *were* thinking of. I really would.'

She lifted her glass and took a mouthful of the wine. Fear gripped her throat, making it difficult to force the wine down. 'It's all in the past,' she said wearily. 'Why keep dredging it up?'

'I know it wasn't a perfect marriage,' he said, his voice low, 'and of course it was tough, having to live on a limited budget in a pretty grotty little house. But we had something, Karen. Something that I would have thought was too good to throw away. What made you do it? Without even giving us a chance to work it out together. Make me understand!' He put his hand on the table, palm up, as though asking her to place her trust in it. His eyes willed her to look at him.

Karen gripped her glass and kept her eyes fixed on the pool of clear liquid in the bottom. She knew she must seem unreasonable, but a cold knot of panic fear was growing tighter and tighter inside her. 'I can't explain. You would never understand.'

He leaned towards her. 'How could you do that to us, Karen? How could you do it to *Holly*?'

She closed her eyes briefly, squeezing them shut. Speaking at random, she said, 'People do it all the time . . .'

His hand suddenly slapped the table. 'I'm not talking about "people"! I'm talking about us! You and me—and our daughter. What sort of woman can walk out and leave a six-month-old baby, without one word of explanation!'

It was the question she had dreaded, the accusation that she had known was coming and could not be avoided. She wanted to get up and run, away from his probing, his anger, his insistence on explanations. Or alternatively, burst into tears and beg for his forgiveness—and she didn't dare. Because he couldn't be expected to forgive her—no man could.

She had to establish some control over herself, the situation. Inwardly she fought a short, tearing battle with hysteria. Then, with the utmost control, 'My sort of woman, evidently,' she said flatly. 'I'd like another drink please—do you mind?' Making a tremendous effort, she raised her eyes and looked expressionlessly into his.

For a moment she thought he was going to refuse. He looked more likely to sweep the glasses from the table and do something violent. But instead he stood up with an impatient exclamation and went back to the bar.

When he returned he put her glass silently in front of her and sat half turned away, sipping at his. She tasted the cool, tart liquid, licked some from her lips, then put the glass down on the table and said softly, 'I'm sorry about your mother, Drew. Truly.'

He didn't reply or respond in any way, and she said, 'What did you do ... about Holly? Who looked after her?'

He threw her a look and sneered. '*Now* you're interested?'

She took a hurried sip of her wine. 'I thought your mother would take her. I was sure ... that she'd be all right.'

'Had it all worked out, did you? Pity you didn't think to consult anyone about those rosy plans of yours.'

'I didn't make any plans!' Her voice cracked, and she put a hand to her face for a moment, but quickly regained her composure. 'I just ... I had to get out, that's all. But I knew that your mother loved Holly and would look after her ...'

'You took a hell of a lot for granted, didn't you? A woman with a heart condition isn't in a fit state to care for a small child.'

'Of course not, but I didn't know that she was ill.'

'Nobody did,' he admitted. 'Not until she had the attack. And I told you, that was shortly after you'd ... left.'

Her eyes widened in sudden horror. 'You mean it was *then*? That's what triggered it?'

Unexpectedly, he shot out his hand to encircle her wrist on the table, holding it in a grip that hurt. '*No*. No, it wasn't your fault. You don't need to blame yourself for that, too.'

She noticed the last word, and smiled ironically. 'You think I have plenty to blame myself for, don't you?'

He took away his hand and leaned back. 'I do happen to think so, yes.'

She was motionless, and after a moment he said, 'That's your cue to ask me if I wasn't to blame, too.'

She shook her head slightly, and he frowned and said, watching her, 'What does that mean?'

'Nothing.'

There was another pause, then he said softly, 'I've lain awake at nights, wondering what it was I did, or didn't do ... what I should have done differently. Of course there were difficulties, but we'd talked them through and accepted them. Hadn't we?' He waited for a reply that didn't come, and finally sighed roughly. 'How much of the blame is mine, Karen?'

She sat with both hands holding her glass on the table, her head bent. 'None of it. You weren't to blame, Drew,' she said huskily. 'It was just ... me.' She wished he wouldn't be like this. It was easier when he was angry, and she could fight him. 'I suppose I was imposing on your mother, expecting her to take over.' Only at the time there hadn't seemed to be any choice. 'I'm sorry, but I thought she would be quite happy to do it. She was such a capable person, and so fond of Holly, even though she never approved of our marriage.'

'She'd accepted it. As you say, she was very fond of her grandchild.' He clenched his fists on the table, and said, 'If you were so unhappy, why didn't you *say* something? *Couldn't you have told me?*'

Mutely, she shook her head again.

A waiter approached and said to Drew, 'Your table is ready now, sir.'

'Oh, good,' Karen said brightly and stood up. Drew gave her a grim look as he took her arm and followed the man to a corner table in the restaurant.

He ordered a bottle of wine to go with their meal, but Karen drank only sparingly. She didn't want him loosening her tongue. While they ate there was little conversation, but over their coffee she asked the question that was uppermost in her mind. 'How is Holly?'

'I thought you'd never ask,' he said drily. 'She's OK. Missing her mother, though.'

'That's ridiculous!' Karen said, shocked. Making her voice cold, she added, 'She can't possibly miss what she's never had.'

'I told you she's looking for a mother figure.'

'She hasn't been to the boutique since that supper.' He smiled faintly. 'Missing her?'

Her heart skipped a beat. 'Of course not. How could I, after all this time?'

'You're disappointed she hasn't come back, though.'

'I only commented because you said she's looking for a mother figure. She did say something about coming to see me, that evening, but as she hasn't, she can't be all that desperate, can she? I didn't really expect her to. And I'm not disappointed.'

'I don't believe you.'

'Believe what you like. I can't be responsible for your sentimental fond imaginings.' Attack, they said, was the best form of defence, but she knew that was unfair, and wished that she hadn't said it.

He put down his cup with a small, sharp clash. 'You wouldn't mind, then, if she found someone else to take your place?'

She actually felt a sharp physical pain in her chest, over her heart, as though someone had hit her there. 'I—told you,' she said, 'that I thought your mother would have done that already.'

'No.'

She said. 'It must have been very difficult for you. Did you ... What did you do?'

'About Holly?'

She nodded.

'At first, of course, my mother had her—for a few weeks. Then, when she got sick, a neighbour of hers stepped in for a while. When Mother's estate was settled I used her insurances to help pay a woman to care for Holly during the day. I inherited the house, too, so I was able to save on rent, and provide a home for the baby. But the woman got another job when her own kids reached school age, and Holly was only two. I had to get someone else. Every arrangement was only temporary, and I had to take more or less what I could get. I wasn't happy about having her cared for by strangers, and eventually I left my job and looked after her myself.'

'*You* did?'

'That's right.'

'But your job——'

'Holly was more important.'

Again the unspoken accusation hovered in the air between them. She thought, You don't understand, you'll never understand. It wasn't because I didn't care ...

So he had left his job, she thought, wrenching her

mind back. The job was not what his mother had wanted for him, but he had been making the most of it. The firm were farm machinery specialists, and there had been good prospects of eventual promotion to a management position involving dealing with overseas contacts, working with government departments in developing countries to improve agricultural methods, and possibly worldwide travel. He would have liked that, with his dual interest in economics and languages. He had intended to make a career in the business, even though it was a second choice, and she was startled to think he had given it up.

She said, 'Did you ever finish your degree?' When they were together, he had been studying hard every night after coming home from work, taking part-time courses towards a diploma in economics.

'Yes. That was an advantage of being at home. I completed most of it part-time and by correspondence, and did the final year after Holly started school.'

'I'm glad you made it,' she told him. He deserved it. He had worked for two years after leaving school to save money to put himself through university, because his mother wasn't able to subsidise the expense. He had really wanted that degree.

He looked at her thoughtfully. 'Thank you. You've made it, too, haven't you? Your own business, selling your own designs. I'd never realised you were so ambitious.'

'I was too young when we met to have formed ambitions. And afterwards——'

'Yes, I know. Is that all it was, Karen? Just that you were so young?'

'Perhaps it was,' she evaded. 'Anyway, the boutique idea wasn't really a long-term ambition. It just sort of . . . evolved. Each step seemed a logical one at the time, and now . . . here I am.'

'And where to from here?'

Lightly, she said, 'Oh, I have no plans to expand. I

like to keep the personal touch, and if the business got bigger I would lose that.'

'So you're content.'

'Yes.'

'And your private life?'

'My private life is my own.'

There was a short, loaded silence. Then he said, 'All right, supposing we bury the past. You might be happy as you are, but my ... position is different. I've got to think about the future.'

'The future?' Karen asked warily.

'Holly's growing up. Soon she'll be a teenager. I'm not sure how I'll cope with an adolescent daughter.'

'You seem to have coped very well so far,' Karen said, sensing danger. 'You've done a good job.'

'It isn't finished yet. The next few years are pretty crucial. It isn't only Holly who thinks she needs a mother figure. I think so, too.'

Karen went cold. Her fingers curled into fists, hidden in her lap. A mother figure. Someone to replace the inadequate mother that she had been. How ironic that apparently only now he had finally decided to divorce her. 'Then I suggest,' she said in brittle tones, 'that you provide one.' Thinking suddenly of the beautiful nightie and the provocative undies he had bought from her, she added, 'I'm sure there's no shortage of suitable candidates.'

His mouth clamped tight. He pushed his cup away and stood up abruptly. 'Let's go.'

She was glad to but, locked in the car with an obviously enraged man, she had second thoughts. Without speaking he drove strictly within the speed limit through the wide streets, his very caution suggesting rigid control over a seething temper.

He stopped with ominous smoothness outside her door, and she was so unnerved that she had difficulty finding the door catch. She was still trying to manipulate it when he went round the outside and opened the door to help her on to the pavement, his fingers digging into the soft flesh of her upper arm.

'You're hurting!' she protested.

He looked down at her and his grip relaxed a little.

Remembering the last time he had seen her home made her even more nervous, and she fumbled as she looked for the key. When she found it, he took it from her, shoved the door open and went in with her.

Turning to face him as he snapped it to behind him and switched on the light, Karen said, 'I don't remember inviting you in.'

'That's because you didn't,' he said, quite pleasantly.

'Then will you please leave?'

'No.'

'I enjoyed the dinner, thank you. Now, I really must ask you to go.'

He suddenly laughed, not nearly so pleasantly. 'Don't push me too far, Karen. I've about had it up to *here* with you treating me as though I'm some total stranger that you're politely trying to get rid of.'

'It may have escaped your notice,' she said, 'but I *am* politely trying to get rid of you.'

He sighed impatiently. 'Do we have to stand here arguing all night?'

'Not if you would just *go!*'

'Oh, the hell with it!' he said disgustedly and, grabbing her arm, propelled her into the lounge. 'Can't we sit down and continue this discussion like two rational adults?'

He pushed her on to the sofa and said, 'Where are the lights?'

Karen leaned over and switched on the table lamp. 'Is that better?' she enquired frostily.

He sat down in the single armchair and regarded her broodingly. 'I hadn't planned on manhandling you,' he said. 'This was meant to be a calm, reasoned discussion.'

'Is that supposed to be an apology?'

He sounded thoroughly fed up. 'I don't want to argue,

Karen. For some reason, every time I see you I end up wanting to wring your neck.'

'There's a simple solution,' she suggested tartly.

'There are two simple solutions, but one's illegal, and the other is impossible.'

She opened her mouth to argue, and he said forcefully, 'Karen, you can't seriously think that I could just say, "Hi, how nice to see you after all this time, and goodbye"!'

Put like that it did sound rather unlikely. 'No,' she acknowledged at last, 'I suppose not.'

'So let's sort out where we go from here,' he suggested almost gently. When she didn't respond, he said, 'I want to tell Holly who you are.'

'*No!*' She almost choked on the word, her body jerking upright. 'You can't!'

'Why not?'

'*Why not?*' She stumbled to her feet. 'For heaven's sake! Dozens of reasons! For one thing, what will it do to her?'

He stood up, watching her. 'Nothing as drastic as what was done to her ten years ago.'

She put a hand to her head and turned away from him. 'Must you keep harping on it?'

Somewhat grittily he said, 'I'm sorry, but that's the whole point, isn't it?'

'What on earth,' she said, swinging round on him fiercely, 'do you think will be gained by telling her at this late stage that she has a mother?'

'She *knows* she has a mother, Karen. She just doesn't know where her mother is.'

Karen whispered, her eyes on his face, 'What did you tell her?'

'I said you had gone away when she was very small, and I didn't know where, or why. I told her the simple truth, that's all. It's one reason why I'd like to be open with her now. I've never deceived her in her life.'

'What does she ... how did she react?'

'She was very young when she first asked, about five.'

About five, Karen thought. The turning point, when I so nearly went back. Supposing I had . . . But Drew was saying, 'She accepted it well, and she's grown up with it. Only lately——'

Without wanting to, Karen asked, 'What?'

'She's been ... unhappy about it. Asking more questions about you, feeling like an odd one out with her friends.'

'Surely some of her friends must have one-parent families? It isn't uncommon.'

'No, but mostly the one parent is the mother. It's . . . unusual for a woman to run out on her family.'

Sensitive to any implied criticism, she said sharply, 'Men have been running out for decades! Why is it different when a woman does it?'

'Let's not get into that,' he said. 'I didn't say it's any different, just that it's not so common. I'm trying to be fair, and not to . . . judge you.' He might be trying, she thought, but she could see the condemnation in his eyes. 'For girls,' he said, 'a mother is important at that age. She *needs* someone, Karen.'

'All *right,* I'm sure you know what she needs.' Mentally she braced herself. 'I suppose you have someone in mind?'

She wouldn't have believed that this could hurt so much. For years she had assumed he had probably found someone else, but now that he was here, talking of it, she could scarcely stop herself from screaming at him.

He was staring at her strangely, his brows drawn together. 'Yes,' he said slowly, 'I have someone in mind.'

She turned away, biting her lip. 'Well, you don't need my permission.'

'Don't you *care?*' He grabbed at her arm suddenly, swinging her round to face him. She could see the baffled anger in his eyes, the pupils contracted as he stared down at her startled face. Then he moved his

other hand, and was gripping her, bringing her closer.
His face had changed, subtly. His eyes darkened, the
pupils growing suddenly larger. She looked away from
them, but her gaze lit on his mouth, and even though it
was closed in a bitter line, she felt a sudden throb of
irrational longing. He said, 'Doesn't it mean anything to
you, that I might be thinking of taking another woman
as my wife . . . and Holly's mother?'

'*Step*mother!' she reminded him involuntarily,
wrenching herself away. Then she said unevenly, 'It's
nothing to do with me.'

'You selfish *bitch*!' he exploded. 'Holly's your *daughter*! Supposing I saddle her with a stepmother she can't
get along with? Someone who doesn't like her! *That's*
nothing to do with you?'

Karen was white, trembling and desperate to hide it.
'You wouldn't do that to her. I wouldn't have left her
with you, if . . .' She looked at him helplessly, her fingers
kneading her temples. She dropped her hand and said, 'I
don't understand why you're telling me all this, what
you're asking me to do.' Surely he didn't expect her to
vet his choice of bride? 'Anyway,' she said huskily, 'I
gave up any rights I have over Holly a long time ago.'

'I know you did,' he said, reining in his temper with
some effort. He paused and said slowly, his eyes on her
face, 'But I'm offering them back to you, Karen.'

CHAPTER FIVE

'WHAT ... do you mean?' she asked through stiff lips, hope and dread a churning mix in her stomach.

For a moment he didn't answer. She had a strange feeling that he had surprised himself. 'I believe the legal term is "access",' he said. 'I'm offering you the chance to see Holly regularly, to have her with you sometimes, to get to know her.'

Her heart began a slow, painful thudding. Her voice muffled, she replied, 'That's ... very generous of you, Drew.'

Harshly he said, 'I'm not doing it for you! This is for her. I told you, she needs someone ... she needs *you*.'

Almost humbly she said, 'I ... Would you trust me?'

His eyes were narrowed and hard. 'There are conditions. You don't say yes unless you can swear you'll stick to the arrangement, that you won't go swanning off again when you get tired of having a daughter.'

Karen felt her face go taut with hurt anger. She turned away to hide it, but he caught her arms again and wrenched her round to face him. 'I want your promise,' he said, 'and if you don't keep to it, if you ever let Holly down again, I swear I'll find you this time and break every damned bone in your beautiful body.' He looked as though he meant it, his eyes unyielding, his voice harsh and threatening. 'And if you don't say yes, I'll do what you wanted—what you said you wanted—and leave you alone. But this is your last chance. You'll never see me— or Holly—again. I'll make sure of it. There are plenty of jobs overseas available to me.'

She stayed still and silent in his hold. His grip was painful, but not nearly as painful as what he was saying. Once she had made the choice, and thought the agony of it would kill her. It had taken years to overcome the crippling damage to her emotions. Now he was asking her to make that same cruel choice over again. She didn't think she had the strength.

Drew said, watching her face, 'You do care for her, Karen. You've tried not to let me know it, but you've shown it a dozen times since we met again. Whatever it was that sent you away, it had nothing to do with Holly. Even after all this time, she isn't just another little girl to you, is she?'

Swallowing, Karen shook her head.

'Whatever you are, whatever you've done in the past, I don't think you'd deliberately hurt her. And she has a right to know her own mother.'

'What about ... if you marry again? Your ... wife might not be very keen on the idea.'

He frowned at her impatiently. 'I'm not marrying again,' he said shortly. 'You jumped to conclusions.'

'Oh.' Disconcerted, she said haltingly, 'I thought you meant ...'

'I know what you thought.' He released her suddenly. 'I don't want to marry anyone else, Karen. Once is enough.'

She looked down at her hands, twisted in front of her. 'I know I must have hurt you ...'

He gave a crack of laughter. 'You have a genius for understatement.'

Her teeth sank painfully into her lower lip, and she moved her head aside.

Drew reached out his hands and took hers in them, loosening her fingers and holding them in a light, firm clasp. Startled, she looked up into his eyes, and found a disturbing light in their depths. 'So what are you going to do about it?' he asked.

She knew he didn't mean Holly. Her own eyes dilated, her blood pounding, and she went rigid, frightened of the power of her feelings, wrenching her gaze away.

Sensing her withdrawal, he tightened his hold on her

hands, making her look at him again. His eyes held hers. 'Karen.'

She shook her head faintly.

At last he loosened his grip and let her step back from him, his eyes unreadable. She thought he was angry again, but after a moment he said, 'All right. If that's how you want to play it.'

She avoided his eyes, trying to appear uncaring.

'What about Holly?' he asked. 'You will see her?'

Suddenly afraid, she searched his face. 'Drew . . . what will she think of me?'

'I can't tell you that,' he said quietly. 'I can only say that everything I've said about you has been good. I told her you were pretty, clever, brave; that you liked strawberries and daffodils and cream cheese and Winnie the Pooh; that you had a nice laugh, and that you made all her baby clothes yourself.'

Her eyes suddenly shimmering with tears, she whispered, 'Thank you. I know I didn't deserve that.' She remembered the bitterness with which he had confronted her that first time, which still broke through in his dealings with her, and was grateful that he had not let it intrude on the picture of her he had presented to their daughter.

'*She* didn't deserve to be told what I really thought of you,' he said.

Karen's eyes widened, and the tears brimmed and slid down her cheeks. She stepped back from him, and he came after her and put his hands on each side of her face and said, roughly, 'No, don't.' His thumbs wiped at the salt moisture on her cheeks, and he said, 'I've hated you, often. There've been times when I could have killed you. Sometimes I thought if I found you, I would do it. And now . . . I'm not sure how I feel . . . Ten years is a long time. You're Karen, and yet you're someone else . . . someone I don't know.' His eyes bored into hers, suddenly fierce, and, perhaps with some idea of appeasing him, she swiftly turned her head until her lips met his palm.

His breath sucked quickly into his chest. '*Karen!*'

He jerked her closer to him, capturing her chin as she closed her eyes, and his lips covered hers, hot and hard.

Desire flared through her, and she welcomed his hands sliding down over her body, curving it to the lines of his until they stood mouth to mouth and thigh to thigh. He brought his hands back to her head and cradled it in his broad palms as his mouth opened hers with raging insistence, and her arms went round him, her fingers urgently caressing his back under his light jacket.

She felt a shudder pass through him, and the kiss became something more as his hands came to her waist, and he locked his arms about her. Her own hands moved to his shoulders and her arms went round his neck, and still their mouths were locked together in a long, intimate, dizzying kiss. When at last he broke it, she dropped her head against his chest, and his lips nuzzled at her nape, sending a delicious shiver of ecstasy down her spine. With his mouth warm and moist on her skin, he muttered, 'Let's go upstairs.'

For a moment longer she lay against him, her pulses thudding, her whole body burning with need. But a faint coldness entered her mind. She stirred, and he loosened his hold a little. Karen opened her eyes and lifted her head. 'What about Holly? Don't you have to be home?'

'She's staying overnight with a friend. She quite often does, when I'm out.'

So that he could stay out all night? The thought intruded and wouldn't be dismissed. He had planned to waylay her tonight after work, he had admitted it. How much further had his plans gone? No, she thought, it wasn't like that. He had wanted to talk to her about Holly's future.

'Karen?' His arms tightened again, and his mouth touched her cheek, sought her mouth again.

But now she resisted, straining away from him. 'No.'

'*No?*' He stared at her averted profile. 'There was an awful lot of yes in that kiss just now.'

She put her hands on his upper arms, determinedly pushing at them. 'I—don't think we should complicate things, do you?' she said feebly.

There was more than a hint of angry frustration in his short laugh, but he let her go.

She raised a shaking hand to her hair, trying to smooth it, and he stood with his hands thrust into his pockets, watching her broodingly. 'Almost like old times, wasn't it, Karen?'

She looked at him fleetingly and didn't answer. It had been an odd blend of familiarity and strangeness. They had known each other's bodies so intimately, and yet they had both changed. His arms were now more muscular and solid, his chest broader, and she knew that he had felt the new slimness of her waist, the less generous but taut contours above and below. Even his kiss had been subtly different. There had been more sureness in the way he held her, in the way his mouth moved over hers, more ... she hesitated over the knowledge, stabbed with sudden jealousy ... more expertise.

'We always sent each other up in flames,' he reminded her. 'There was never any problem in bed. Though that's another thing I've wondered ... whether you were pretending, after all.'

She still didn't answer, though her face flamed, and he said abruptly, 'All right. Leave it. You will see Holly, won't you?'

'If ... she wants to see me.'

'I don't think there's any hidden resentment in *her*. She'll be curious, of course. Just remember what I said, and promise me one thing ...'

'Yes?'

He looked at her consideringly and said, 'Don't lie to her. Say so if you don't want to answer some of her questions, but don't tell lies. I never have. She's been brought up to trust in a parent's word.'

'I promise I won't.'

He waited a moment, then said, 'OK. Fine. I'll contact you and let you know, after I've told Holly. Do you want me there, or would you prefer to be alone with her?'

Hesitantly, she said, 'If you don't mind, I think I'd prefer to see her alone.'

'OK.' The word was a trifle clipped. 'If that's what you want . . . unless Holly expresses a strong preference otherwise, of course.'

'Yes, of course.' Holly's preference must be the deciding factor. She quite understood that.

'Well, that's it, then,' he said. 'Goodnight, Karen.' He didn't go immediately, but stood waiting for her response.

'Goodnight,' she said woodenly.

There was a hint of mockery in the smile he gave her before he turned towards the door.

It wasn't until she had made herself a strong cup of coffee, and finished it, that she realised the fabric she had been going to cut out was still in Drew's car. Anyway, she told herself, it didn't really matter. She was far too wrung out to concentrate on the task tonight. She would just go to bed with a good book, instead.

Drew brought the parcel into the shop the following day, just as she was about to take her lunch break. 'I hope you didn't miss it too much,' he said. 'I only found it this morning as I was on my way to work.'

'It doesn't matter. I'll take it home again tonight.'

'I could pick you up.'

'No, thanks.' She didn't want to make a habit of it.

'Have lunch with me?'

Had he spoken to Holly? She looked at him, trying to assess his expression, asking him with her eyes to give her some signal. She glanced at Gretta, who was hovering nearby, all ears, while pretending to sort a rack of dressing-gowns into order.

He said, 'Well?' giving her no help, and finally she answered, 'Yes, all right. I'll just get my bag.'

Gretta said cheerfully as she went out, 'Don't hurry back, I'll be OK.'

Karen didn't answer, but Drew said, 'Thanks,' as he took her arm at the door.

The street was crowded, and Drew walked fast. It wasn't until they were seated at a table in the restaurant he had chosen that she was able to ask, 'Have you talked to her?'

There was slight surprise in his glance. 'I haven't seen her yet. Remember I told you she stayed with a friend last night?'

'Oh! Yes.' Some of the tension went out of her. 'Why did you ask me to lunch, then?'

With laughter in his voice, he said, 'Do I need an excuse to invite a beautiful woman to have lunch with me?'

'I'm not a beautiful woman,' she said, 'I'm——'

'Yes?' he prompted.

She had been about to say, 'I'm your wife.' And of course she couldn't say that. 'I'm . . . the mother of your child,' she said.

'All the more reason,' he said. 'And you *are* a beautiful woman. Even more so, I think, than you were.'

'Thank you.' The compliment made her uneasy, and she stared down at the salad before her, stirring the lettuce with her fork. 'You said I was too thin.'

'I said you'd lost weight. And before we start a marital argument, that does not mean you were too fat before.'

A marital argument. It made them sound like any ordinary married couple, having a mild wrangle over their lunch, and going home together afterwards to a familiar house, later sleeping together in a familiar double bed.

'I'm older,' she said.

'So am I. And you're only twenty-eight. I don't see a lot of wrinkles, or grey hairs.'

'I'll have them, eventually.'

He gave a breath of laughter. 'And I'll be bald and pot-bellied.'

She looked at him, unable to imagine it. 'No,' she said, 'you'll be a distinguished older man.'

He raised his brows and bowed an acknowledgement. 'And you'll be a mature beauty.'

'Men weather better than women.'

'Does it bother you?' he asked. 'Getting older?'

'Sometimes.' There had been times when she wondered what she was going to do for the rest of her life, a married woman without a husband, a mother without a child. The years ahead had stretched bleak and empty.

But now, there was Holly ... and Drew. For a moment hope lifted her heart. Was it possible ...?

Foolish daydreams, she chided herself. There was no going back. No chance of regaining the years they had lost, that she had deliberately renounced.

'When will you talk to her?' she asked.

'Before the weekend. Will you be home then?'

'At the weekend? Yes.'

She would have cancelled everything, anyway, if there was a chance that Holly would come.

'I may bring her round then.'

'Yes, all right.'

He pushed away his plate and picked up his cup of coffee. 'Of course, she might need to think about it,' he said. 'But if I know Holly, she'll be agog to see you.'

Her eyes flew to his face. 'Do you think so?'

He put down the cup. 'Yes, I do.' Slowly, he added, 'You really want this, don't you? You want it to work out.'

Her painfully intense gaze fell away from his. 'Yes,' she said, barely audible.

He leaned towards her. 'It may not be all roses, you know. Holly's a good kid, but she's no saint. And I'm not quite sure how all this will affect her.'

Suddenly apprehensive, for Holly's sake as well as her own, she looked at him accusingly. 'You seemed very sure of yourself the other night! You kept telling me this was what she needed.'

'I'm sure she ought to know you. Good or bad, I think that everyone has a basic human right to know where they come from and who their parents are. It just doesn't seem right that she should have a mother living in the same city, and not see her. If she found out later, and I hadn't—hadn't let you see her, she'd have every right to blame me for not doing this. But I can't tell just how she'll react. Nobody can.'

'I'm ... scared,' she confessed. 'I'm dead scared.'

'I guess so. I'm a bit scared, myself. But for her sake I think we should minimise the drama as far as we can. Try to be fairly casual about it all.'

'Casual!' Her whole body was shaking, just at the thought of meeting her daughter again. Which was silly. She had already seen her three times, and had managed to treat her—almost—like any other chance-met child.

'Just try,' Drew suggested.

And she said, 'Yes, I will.'

He phoned on Sunday, just after nine. She went flying to lift the receiver, certain it was him, hardly waiting for him to say so before asking breathlessly, 'What did she say? Is she coming?'

'We're both coming,' he told her.

'Oh.' Because Holly had asked him to accompany her, of course.

'She's had a sudden attack of shyness,' he explained.

Holly, who was about the most un-shy of youngsters, was nervous of meeting her mother now that she knew who she was! Karen's throat ached in sympathy. She felt overwhelmed with a guilty depression.

'We'll be over in about an hour, if that's all right?' Drew said.

An hour. An age. What could possibly take them so long?

'Yes,' she said. 'An hour will be fine.'

She had already vacuumed, dusted and unnecessarily cleaned, picked up cushions, plumped them absently and put them down again. She had even made a batch of peanut brownies, although she hadn't baked in years. It hadn't been very successful, and she didn't think trying again would improve matters. Now she raced up the stairs to check her reflection in the mirror, making sure her hair was properly secured in its neat roll, and wondering if fitting cord pants and a muslin blouse were suitable gear, or if she ought to change. What would Holly expect her to be wearing?

'Nothing, you idiot,' she said to her reflection, and then giggled with a hint of hysteria at herself. 'Anything,' she amended. Holly probably wouldn't even notice.

But when she opened the door to their ring, it appeared that Holly did notice. Karen said, 'Hello,' and gripped the doorknob and then released it, making a clumsy half-gesture towards her daughter, but Holly stood with Drew's hands on her shoulders and gravely stared. Her eyes examined Karen's face first, then her clothes, and returned to her face, and Karen was unable to decipher any emotion except curiosity. She dropped her hands and said, 'Please ... come in.'

She led the way to the lounge, and Holly stayed close to her father and sat beside him on the sofa. She was wearing a dirndl skirt and an embroidered blouse, and her long hair was tied in a ponytail with a pink ribbon. Karen thought, achingly, how pretty she was, and wondered who had chosen her clothes.

'Would you like something to drink?' Karen asked them. 'There's fruit juice or lemonade ... and tea and coffee.'

'Holly?' Drew prompted.

Looking only at him, she said, 'Lemonade, please.'

'I'd like coffee,' Drew said.

'Yes, of course.'

She fled into the kitchen, leaning over the sink, feeling suddenly sick. It wasn't going to work. Holly hated her. They were strangers. How could anyone expect them to establish a normal relationship after all this time?

She took a deep breath and put on the electric jug, and poured some lemonade into a long glass. With shaking fingers, she cut a lemon and placed a slice on the side of the glass, and added a striped straw and a couple of ice cubes. She made coffee for herself and Drew and placed all three drinks on a tray with a plateful of peanut brownies. She could hear Drew speaking quietly, but couldn't make out the words. He stopped and looked up as she came back to the lounge, and stood up to take the tray from her and place it on the coffee table.

Trying to sound friendly and normal, Karen said, 'I hope you like peanut brownies, Holly.'

'Yes, thank you,' the child said politely. She took one from the plate, and lifted the lemonade from the tray.

Drew said, 'That looks very grown-up.'

Holly sipped, and this time threw a quick look at Karen. 'It's very nice, thank you.'

Karen tried a smile. 'I'm glad you like it.'

'Did you make these?' Drew took a brownie and bit into it.

'Yes.' She took her coffee and sat in the armchair.

'Mm. Delicious.'

'Thank you. They're not very good,' she said absently, more to Holly than to him. 'They spread all over the oven tray.'

'You probably used too much butter,' Drew said.

Startled, she looked away from Holly and into his face. He appeared to be serious. Of course, if he had spent several years caring for a child, it was logical he should have tried his hand at making biscuits.

He was trying to hold her eyes, a message telegraphing

from his own, and she suddenly understood. She had focused all her attention on Holly, and the child wasn't ready for it. Relax, his eyes said, let her take her time. Let's just ignore her for a while.

Some of the tension left her, and she settled deeper into her chair, keeping her gaze carefully away from Holly, who was concentrating on her drink. She said, 'I followed the recipe.'

'Recipes are fine,' Drew answered gravely, 'but it depends on the stove too, some ovens are a bit fierce, and you need to use a lower temperature than the recipe says.'

It was an inane conversation, but it was giving Holly a breathing space, and Karen was grateful to Drew for initiating it. After a while the subject switched to television programmes, and eventually Holly spoke directly to Karen. 'Please may I have another brownie?'

'Yes, of course.' Karen nodded and went on talking to Drew, and as Holly was licking the crumbs from about her mouth, Drew said '. . . and Holly won't miss *Ready To Roll* if she can help it.' He turned to her and said, 'Eh, chicken? At top decibel level whenever possible.'

Holly made a face at him. 'It's no good if you can't *feel* the music! And I *won't* damage my ears, just listening to the TV!'

'Well, your mother and I felt much the same about our music, didn't we?' He turned to Karen. 'But it's the function of the older generation to disapprove of the next one's music.'

'You don't really disapprove, Daddy, you only pretend to. Do *you* like modern music?' she appealed to Karen.

From then on it was easier. Holly chatted almost normally, and later wandered over to Karen's work table and showed a curiosity about what she used it for. Drew remained silently watching from the sofa as Karen explained how she took inspiration from the fabric samples and created designs to suit.

At eleven-thirty, Drew said, 'Time we were going. Karen will be wanting her lunch.'

Karen glanced at Holly, and said, 'Can you stay? I can boil some eggs. Or there's soup.'

'Another time,' Drew said easily. 'We have a date to go fishing with some friends, and we've got to get home and change.'

She shouldn't have been hurt. She didn't point out that they would presumably have to lunch somewhere, and that it wouldn't take more than ten minutes to make it for them. But they had a life apart from hers, and Drew was making that clear.

This was what was meant by 'access'. She could have her child for visits by pre-arrangement, but there were other visits, other activities, even other people, in Holly's life that meant as much, perhaps more. She didn't seem at all reluctant to leave. And Drew would always have the right of saying, we must go. She must go. She can only stay for so long. You can have her for an hour, or two hours, perhaps a day. But she comes back to me.

After they had gone, she slowly put the rest of the peanut brownies in a tin, and washed the dishes. It had gone off well, really, she told herself. She was lucky that Drew was so understanding, so willing for her to see Holly at all. He might have been vindictive. But it wasn't for Karen's sake that he was encouraging contact between them. He had made it quite obvious that his only motive was Holly's happiness. That was all that counted with him. It was a laudable motive, but for some reason it created in Karen an unutterable and inexplicable depression.

The next visit was easier. Drew only stayed a few minutes before leaving them alone, and after a few awkward moments, Holly saw that Karen had been working on a new design, and asked if she could watch. After a while, she said, 'I think a frill round the hem would be nice,' and Karen drew it in, and they spent the remainder of the afternoon happily swapping suggestions and incorporating them in designs.

Karen began to look forward to the weekends, and plan things for them to do. Spring was turning into summer, and sometimes they left the flat and went walking and she showed Holly the places she had visited on her own when she first came to the city. One day they took some stale bread and fed the ducks in the Domain. A couple of times Drew said they had other plans, and Holly didn't come at all. Karen spent the entire weekend wondering what they were doing, and feeling sorry for herself and horribly left out.

Drew came into the shop late one afternoon and said, 'I've promised to take Holly to a film tonight. She'd like you to come, too. Are you free?'

She was, but she hesitated. This was a new development, the three of them going out like a family.

Drew said, 'Take pity on me, Karen. It's one of those *Star Wars* fantasy movies. I could do with another adult to share it with. Besides, if you're going to play the mother role you'd better get used to the idea of tolerating your kid's tastes in music and movies.'

She looked at him warily, but there didn't seem to be anything but humour in his face, and somehow she found herself accepting. The movie wasn't so bad, and she was rash enough to say so later, and had to endure his teasing about her juvenile bad taste. Afterwards they took her home and she invited them in and gave them toasted crumpets for supper. Holly was sparkling, enjoying having them both together, and Drew was relaxed and companionable. Karen hadn't enjoyed herself so much for years.

At the boutique the Christmas rush was starting, business was brisk and she was staying up late at night preparing her Christmas stock. When Drew brought Holly in to her on the second weekend in December, he said, 'You look tired. What have you been doing to yourself?'

'I've been working, that's all. It's nearly Christmas, our busiest time of the year.'

He gave her a sharp look, but said nothing. When he picked up Holly later in the day, though, he sent her out to the car and said to Karen as she stood in the doorway, 'Do you take a break at Christmas?'

'Yes. I'm closing the shop for the statutory holidays, of course.'

'Must you open between Christmas and New Year? A lot of smaller businesses don't. Surely you don't do a lot of trade in your line directly after Christmas.'

'No,' she admitted, tempted by the idea of a long break. 'Mostly we get college girls, just browsing. Still . . . it's a long time to close down.'

'Only three shopping days. What are you going to miss?'

Possibly half a dozen sales, she supposed, at that time. Most people had spent their money on Christmas presents. Certainly trade would be slack.

'We're going to a beach up north for Christmas,' Drew said. 'Come with us.'

She couldn't speak for a moment, too surprised to even think.

'A family Christmas,' he said. 'Holly doesn't remember ever having one.'

The idea was compelling, but she was almost frightened by the implications. 'I need to think about it,' she temporised.

'You owe it to her, Karen.'

Blackmail, she thought, flashing him a wary glance. 'I said, I'll think about it.'

By the following weekend she still hadn't decided. Holly had run to the car but Drew lingered on the doorstep, asking Karen, 'Have you thought about that holiday?'

'You haven't mentioned it to Holly, have you?'

'No. It's tempting . . .'

'That would be unfair.'

'True. Sometimes I wonder if I'm a fool to play fair with you.'

It was a long time since he had sniped at her, and the unexpected gibe went home. She dropped her eyes to hide the hurt in them.

'You'd sleep with Holly, of course,' he said, and she looked up, startled.

'I hadn't expected . . .'

'To sleep with me? I didn't think so . . . But I don't know why you're hesitating.'

She wasn't sure, either, except that she seemed to be getting deeper and deeper into something she had never planned to happen. Before, she had persuaded herself that she had made her life bearable, even interesting if unexciting, a smooth surface underlaid by a deeply buried ache so constant that she scarcely even noticed it. Now her moods alternated between a singing happiness and a premonition of impending disaster. The happiness had a precarious quality to it, as though in her heart she knew it couldn't last. And it was never quite enough.

'It would do you good,' he said. 'You need a holiday, by the look of you.'

'Thanks,' she said tartly.

She stared beyond him and saw Holly sitting in the car, her face turned curiously in their direction. Drew followed her glance, and looked at her again. 'You know she'd love you to come,' he said. 'It's been good for her, Karen,' he added, almost reluctantly. 'It was the right thing to do.'

'You sound relieved.'

'I had second thoughts once or twice,' he said. 'You'd let us both down once. I've often told myself I was mad, inviting you to do it again . . .'

'You made me promise . . .'

'Yes. But how much have promises ever meant to you?'

Karen drew a sharp breath. 'You believe in being brutally frank, don't you?'

'Does that sting? Maybe it should. I thought this was what Holly needed, I'd been vaguely searching for some kind of honorary aunt or housekeeper . . . and it seemed stupid and unnecessarily complicated to look around for someone to take her mother's place, just when her mother had providentially turned up. I guess I thought fate had taken a hand. But I wasn't sure that it would work out.' He paused. 'You don't know what it's like. Being totally responsible for another human being, always worrying if you're doing the right thing, or causing some irreparable damage through sheer bloody ignorance.'

'I *do* know!' she blazed at him, suddenly savage. '*How dare you stand there and tell me I don't know!*'

Disconcerted, he stared at her. Then anger of his own kindled in his eyes. 'Do you really think six months compares with ten *years*?' he demanded incredulously.

It didn't, of course. And he didn't have any idea of the pressures that had driven her to walk out on them. Sullenly, she said, 'No, I suppose not. You'd better go. Holly's waiting.'

As if to bear her out, Holly leaned from the car window and said plaintively, 'Dad—dy!'

'All right!' he called impatiently. 'I'm coming.'

Karen moved back into the doorway. 'Will I see you next week?'

'Yes. And you'd better have an answer for me. And it had better be yes!'

In the end it was yes. Not, she told herself, because of anything he had said, but simply because she wanted to spend the time with Holly, and she knew it would please the child, too.

She had bought for Holly a set of real gold bangles which were simple but had cost quite a lot of money, and a large, exquisite musical doll in Spanish costume that

Holly had admired in a shop window. But the most important present was a set of underwear in handwoven silk and worked with an embroidered design and handmade lace trimming. Every stitch Karen had put in herself, working lovingly over the design and its execution to create something uniquely pretty and perfect.

She also had a present for Drew, and she placed it in one of the boutique's gift boxes before he and Holly picked her up on Christmas Eve after the shop had closed.

CHAPTER SIX

WHILE Holly huddled on the back seat with a blanket and pillow, Drew took the car over the Harbour Bridge and out of the city. The traffic was heavy, and for the first half-hour progress was slow, but gradually the flow thinned somewhat, although there were obviously hundreds of motorists with their families leaving the city to spend their Christmas Day elsewhere. Holly had gone to sleep by the time they reached Albany and left the wide straight motorway.

At Orewa, the main street that was also the highway was still alive with people, and several cars turned into the popular camping ground on the foreshore where tents and caravans were cheek by jowl with one another. Drew slowed the car almost to a crawl, picking up speed a little as they climbed the steep incline past the long beach. Looking back past his shoulder, Karen could see a host of lights, and the pale ribbon of sand with the sea's edge rippling whitely on to it.

She lifted a hand to stifle a yawn, and Drew said, 'Tired?'

'A bit. It's been a hectic week.'

'The seat goes back, if you'd like to try and sleep.'

'No, thanks. It would only make me dopey.'

'It's quite a long trip. Especially in this traffic.'

'Never mind. I'm used to late nights.'

'A full social life?' There was a slight edge to his voice. Or perhaps she had imagined it.

'No,' she said, carefully non-committal.

'Work, is it?'

'Mostly, yes.'

'Is that really necessary, Karen?'

'I enjoy it.'

'You must have some recreation.'

'I do. I read a lot, and go for long walks, and . . . see friends.'

'You do have some, then?'

'Of course I do,' she said somewhat coldly.

'I wondered. Holly's never mentioned visiting anyone with you, or you having visitors.'

She had wanted every precious moment with Holly to herself. Besides, none of her friends knew about her marriage, and she didn't especially want to explain the sudden advent of an eleven-year-old daughter into her life.

She shrugged. 'I don't suppose Holly has told you every detail of what we do together, anyway.'

He looked at her for a moment. 'Pretty well,' he informed her.

She frowned. 'Have you been cross-examining her about my life?'

He threw a glance over his shoulder to see Holly fast asleep in the corner of the back seat. Keeping his voice low, he said, 'Don't be so touchy. Holly and I have a pretty close relationship, and she's somewhat over-whelmed by the novelty of having you in her life. She chatters when she comes home after visiting you. I don't need to "cross-examine" her—even if I were interested.'

Her cheeks stung, and she looked the other way, staring out at the moonlit landscape as they traversed a high ridge where the hills fell away on each side of the road and pale water glimmered far below.

It was a long time before they spoke again. The road turned inland, passed through several small towns, and wound up into the Brynderwyn hills. Eventually they came to the summit and looked down on the wide sweep of the distant sea, washed colourless in moonlight, with

the jet flare of flame marking the oil refinery at Marsden
Point.

'I always feel we're nearly there when we get to this
place,' Drew remarked. He glanced at his watch. 'Just
after eleven o'clock. We should be in Whangarei in time
to catch a midnight carol service. OK?'

She had always avoided going to church at Christmas.
It hadn't been a time of celebration for her, but a period
of grief and deep depression. The carols, the emphasis
on family, above all the ubiquitous images of the Christ-
child, had sent her howling for cover. She was always
glad when it was over at last.

But this year was different. Even if it never happened
again, she would have this memory to treasure. 'Oh,
yes!' she said softly. 'That's a lovely idea.'

Holly sat between them in the church, blinking
sleepily at first, but eager to take part, sharing a song
sheet with Karen as they joined in singing the carols, and
tugging her down to the front of the church afterwards
to see the crib that had been set up there.

When they had returned to the car, Holly said, 'It's
Christmas Day, isn't it?'

'That's right.'

'Merry Christmas, Daddy!' She was bubbling, leaning over the seat to plant a kiss on his cheek.

He reciprocated in kind, and Holly turned to Karen
and said, 'Merry Christmas . . . Mummy.'

She had never called Karen that before. Usually she
avoided naming her at all, and if she did, she said
'Karen'.

Karen turned, and warm, childish lips pressed against
her skin. She put her hand on Holly's face, and said
shakily, 'Merry Christmas, darling,' and for the first
time in ten years, kissed her daughter.

Holly bounced back into the corner, did up her safety-
belt on Drew's order, and cocooned herself in the
blanket.

Drew started the car, and Karen sat wrapped in a new and precious warmth, going over in her mind every moment since they had first stepped into the church and heard the organ playing 'Silent Night'.

This was how it might have been, all those years. The three of them loving, sharing, being together ... a family. This was how it should have been, would have, but for her ...

The car sped further north, and she stared at the darkness leaping away ahead of them in front of the headlights, and saw nothing but memories, bitter and sweet. She didn't even know that she was crying until she heard Drew say quietly, 'Don't!' And his hand came out and covered hers, holding it tight.

She lifted her other hand and wiped at the tears, and after a while they stopped. Drew didn't relinquish his hold until he had to turn off the main road and they lost the tarmac. He drove slowly round sharp curves on the metal road, steeply uphill, and then down towards the coast, and eventually stopped the car in front of a small, squat house that stood slightly apart from a dozen others fronting the shoreline.

He glanced at Holly, who had gone to sleep again, and undid his seat-belt and Karen's. Karen made to get out, but he stopped her, turning her face towards him with a firm hand. 'Are you all right?' he asked her, his voice low.

Karen nodded, but he didn't let her go at once. The moonlight floated in through the windscreen and showed him her face, a pale oval against the restraining curve of his hand. 'Merry Christmas, Karen,' he said, and bent to kiss her, his lips gentle, questioning.

She sat very still, allowing his exploration of her pliant mouth, but not responding. She was very tired and emotionally drained. The kiss was comforting, and she wanted nothing more.

He lifted his head and sat back, regarding her for a

moment before he said, 'We'll get the bags inside and make a bed for Holly before we wake her.'

Karen made up the two single beds in one of the bedrooms, and unpacked from Holly's case the nightie she had made for the girl's birthday. Drew put Karen's case at the foot of the other bed and said, 'OK?'

'Yes, you can bring her in now.'

Holly refused Karen's offer to help her undress, but was soon tucked in and asleep again. As Karen quietly opened her own case, Drew tapped on the door. 'Karen? Want a cup of something?'

She opened the door and said, 'No, thanks. I'll go straight to bed.'

'OK. The bathroom's over there. I'm falling into bed, too.' He went past her to look down at Holly for a moment, and stooped to drop a featherlight kiss on the child's cheek.

Karen stayed by the door watching, and as he passed her again on his way out, he suddenly smiled and, bending close, brushed his lips over her cheek, too. 'Goodnight,' he said. 'Sleep well.'

She did, but not as late as she might have expected. When she woke, her watch said eight o'clock, and the other bed was empty. She could hear voices in the outer room that was a combination kitchen-dining-living area, and from outside the squawk of seagulls mingling with the murmur and shush of waves washing on the beach.

She slipped into the bathroom and had a shower, then dressed quickly in jeans and a pink cotton shirt, used a minimum of make-up and combed out her hair. She hesitated, then plaited the fine strands again and secured the end with an elastic band.

When she entered the other room, Holly was sitting at the table buttering toast, and she traced the delicious smell of frying bacon to the stove where Drew was about to break an egg into the pan. Looking up he said, 'Good morning. One egg or two?'

'One, thank you. Can I help?' She was bemusedly looking at the centrepiece on the table, a small pine tree in a yellow plastic bucket of sand, the branches hung with tinsel and tiny Christmas bells.

'Everything's under control,' Drew said. 'Sit down, and have some cornflakes if you like.'

Karen sat down and fingered a delicate silver bell. 'Where on earth did all this come from?'

He glanced up from the pan and said, 'We brought it with us, in the boot of the car.'

'It got a bit squashed, with all the luggage,' Holly said, 'but it looks better now. We had to have a tree, didn't we, Daddy?'

'Can't have Christmas without a tree,' he agreed, lifting a rasher of crisp bacon from the pan. 'And after breakfast we'll put the presents on the table, too.'

Karen helped Holly wash up when they had eaten, and afterwards she fetched the parcels she had brought and placed them with the other packages round the little Christmas tree.

'Can we open them now?' Holly asked.

Drew exchanged a glance of amusement with Karen, and said, 'I guess so. Go ahead.'

He moved to the sofa against one wall, bringing Karen with him by a gentle pressure on her waist, and sat with his arm behind her shoulders.

Holly picked up a parcel and said, 'This one's yours, Daddy. And this one's for ... Mummy. And here's another one for you,' she said to Karen and brought them over, then danced back to the table to find another parcel for her father before picking up all those with her own name on them, sitting cross-legged at her parents' feet while she opened them all. Drew had given her a book, several tapes of her favourite pop groups, and a transistorised tape player with earphones. 'To save my hearing,' he joked, as Holly thanked him with an extravagant hug. 'Spoilt brat. Go on, you've got some more presents, yet.'

'Oh, thank you!' she said to Karen, jingling the bangles along her arm. 'They're neat!' The doll met with equivalent appreciation, and the set of underclothes had to be tried on immediately.

'They're lovely,' Drew said. 'Look after them.'

'I will.' She sat down again, still wearing the frilled petticoat, and said, 'Now it's your turn, Daddy.'

Karen had already seen the desk diary Holly had bought him, and the pencil holder she had painstakingly made from a jam jar covered with scraps of cloth in a patchwork pattern. He thanked Holly enthusiastically and, turning to the third parcel on his lap, opened the box and lifted out the beautifully fashioned raw silk shirt, with the small monogram of his initials embroidered in tan thread on the pocket, and a matching handkerchief tucked into it.

'You *made* this?' he asked Karen.

'Yes. I hope you like it.'

'Of course I like it,' he said. 'It's ... terrific. Thank you.' He leaned over and dropped a quick kiss on her lips. 'I hope you like yours, though I'm afraid I'm not clever enough to make anything for you myself.'

Karen opened Holly's present first, expressing a genuine pleasure and admiration over the carefully worked pin cushion and the diary similar to Drew's, and then tugged at the ribbon on the last small package.

It was a jeweller's box, and when she opened it she caught her breath. There was a ring with an amber stone in a graceful gold setting, and a pair of matching ear-rings, amber teardrops on fine gold hooks.

'I hope it fits,' Drew said coolly, and he removed the ring and took her right hand, and pushed the gold circlet on to the third finger.

He eased it down over the knuckle and said, 'It's all right, isn't it?'

'Yes,' she said, her face white. 'It's . . . perfect. Thank you.'

'Put on the ear-rings,' Holly urged.

Drew picked them up, and she removed the tiny sleepers she was wearing and replaced them with the ear-rings.

Holly said, 'They're beautiful, aren't they?'

'Yes,' Karen said. 'What are the stones?'

'Topaz,' Drew told her. 'Do you like them?'

'Yes. Very much. But . . . this set must have been expensive.'

'It's a long time since I bought you a present,' he said, and stood up. 'Who wants a walk on the beach?' he said easily. 'We've been here——' he glanced at his watch, '—nearly nine hours already, and we haven't even sniffed at the sea.'

Holly ran to change her clothes, and Karen followed her more slowly, taking off the ring and the ear-rings to replace them in their box, leaving it on the dressing-table.

The sand was clean and white, and the sea rippled in along the wide crescent, breaking round a small, steep islet at one end of the beach where a fisherman perched with his rod, the tide tugging at his line.

Holly, dressed now in red shorts and a vest, ran ahead, splashing in and out of the waves, and stopping now and then to examine some intriguing flotsam thrown up on the sand.

Drew, barefoot and with his jeans rolled up above his ankles, took Karen's hand in his and lifted it. 'You've taken the ring off?'

'It's a dress ring, isn't it?' she said. 'I wouldn't want to damage it.'

She tried to remove her hand from his, but his fingers were firm, and he retained his hold as they walked. There was a faint breeze, and scudding clouds overhead, and as one of them covered the sun Karen shivered.

'Cold?' Drew asked.

'Not really,' she answered hastily, but he let go her hand and put his arm about her instead, and she felt the warm weight of it on her shoulders.

Holly was bending over something at the edge of the waves, touching it tentatively with a short stick. She turned to them and beckoned, and Karen quickened her pace, slipping away from Drew to go and see what was holding Holly's interest.

'Look!' Holly said as they came nearer. 'It's a sea-egg. It's still got its spines, but I think it's dead.'

The hedgehog-like object turned over as a wave sucked at it, and Drew bent to pick it up. A strong stench arose from it, and Holly said 'Pooh!' and made a face.

'It's whole, though,' Karen pointed out. 'If it was cleaned out and dried the spines would fall off and the shell would be really pretty.'

Holly wrinkled her face dubiously, and Drew laughed and made to throw the thing out to sea.

'No, don't!' Karen objected. 'Give it to me.'

She took it from him, ignoring his sceptical look, and walked into the waves, where she allowed the water to wash out the rotten matter through the small hole in the bottom. Some of the spines began to come off, too, and she picked off more and rubbed the others away on the sand before washing the whole thing again. They came of quite easily, and the blue-green and reddish shades of the underlying pattern began to show through.

Drew had rinsed his hand in the waves, and he and Holly had wandered further along the beach. When they turned and strolled back to her, she held out the thoroughly cleaned object in her hand and said triumphantly, 'See?'

'It still pongs a bit,' Holly said critically.

'It won't once it dries out properly,' Karen assured her. 'It'll be beautiful.'

'Mmm.' Holly looked doubtful, waving a hand in

front of her nose to show that she still found the odour offensive, before she went running off towards the house.

Karen sniffed at her fingers. 'I'm afraid I pong a bit, too,' she said.

'You didn't need to go quite that far,' Drew told her.

Uncertain of his meaning, she looked at him, to see a gleam of humour in his eyes. 'I must say the perfume's unusual. I suppose,' he said, 'it is one way of keeping a man at bay.'

'I'll wash my hands when we get back,' she assured him. 'And spray them with eau-de-Cologne, if you like.'

He cocked his head, teasing. 'Does that mean I'll be allowed to hold them again?'

Suddenly light-hearted, she said, 'I'm not stopping you!'

She hadn't expected him to take her up on that, but he immediately possessed himself of her hand and linked his fingers into hers.

'You'll stink!' she warned him.

'I don't care. Perhaps it's like eating onions. If both of us smell of it, neither of us will notice it.'

'Holly will.'

'Well,' he drawled, 'that could have its advantages. There are times when an eleven-year-old is a slight handicap to certain activities.'

He was looking for her reaction, but she wasn't prepared for this. She looked away from him and said hastily, 'She's already there. We'd better hurry.'

'She can wait,' he said, holding her back as she tried to quicken their pace, but Holly was calling, and as they approached she said, 'Can I go for a swim, Daddy?'

Drew looked at the sky and said, 'Is it warm enough?'

'Yes, yes!' She hopped from one foot to the other, and Drew smiled resignedly, and said, 'Well, I suppose you'll come out if you're cold.'

'Come with me!' she begged, but he said firmly, 'No.

You can swim if Karen will keep an eye on you, but I'm going to get the dinner on.'

He opened the door and a delicious smell greeted them.

Surprised, Karen said, 'Roast chicken?'

'I put it on before breakfast,' Drew informed her. 'Christmas dinner, no less.'

'I'm impressed,' she admitted.

Holly was tugging at her arm. 'Come swimming with me, Karen ... Mummy?'

'Watch her,' Drew advised. 'She's a champion wheedler when she wants something.'

Karen laughed. 'I don't mind supervising, but I'll save the swim for later, thanks.'

She stayed on the beach while Holly splashed about along with a number of other people who had decided to brave the water, and later they sat down to roast chicken and potatoes, kumara and peas, followed by strawberries and ice cream.

After the dishes were done, they found the sun had come out in earnest, and Karen and Drew spent the afternoon lazing on the sand, occasionally being persuaded by a more energetic Holly to join her in a swim. There were a lot of people about now, and once Drew waved to someone in the distance whom he evidently knew, but he didn't leave Karen's side to go and speak to them.

Karen made chicken and salad sandwiches for tea, and they sat on the steps to eat them, admiring the view and enjoying the long summer evening. Karen had caught the sun, in spite of using sunscreen lotion, and her arms and cheeks burned faintly. Her hair had loosened from its plait, and untidy strands wafted across her face so that she had to keep stroking them back with her fingers, and she had no make-up left at all. But she had had a wonderful day, and she couldn't be bothered tidying up. Anyway, she thought, looking at the other two, they looked at least as disreputable. Holly's ponytail had slipped sideways and gone lank with dampness, and her toes were caked with sand. Drew had got the legs of his jeans wet somehow and had discarded his shirt entirely, and his hair was windblown.

Holly was yawning by eight-thirty, although it was still light, and Drew packed her, with very little protest, off to bed. He had opened a bottle of white wine at lunchtime, and there was still some left. He poured two glasses and offered Karen one, and they sat on together in silence. Now that Holly was gone, she imagined that the atmosphere had subtly changed. She felt Drew's eyes on her as she sipped at the wine, and studiously avoided them. But when she had finished, he took the glass and put it with his just inside the door, and stood up. 'Come for a walk,' he said.

Karen hesitated, suddenly remembering a remark he had made this morning about children being inhibiting. As if reading her mind, he bent and tugged her up beside him, holding her wrist. 'Come on,' he said. 'I won't do anything to hurt you.'

'What about Holly?'

'She'll be all right. This place is as safe as houses. Most of the families come here year after year. Tomorrow there'll be a few more. A lot of people spend Christmas Day at home, before coming up here.'

'Do you own the house?' she asked as he closed the door behind them.

'Yes. I bought it a few years ago.'

'I thought you'd only moved to Auckland recently.'

'About a year ago. I had a job with a dairy company in the north, running their retail division, after I finished my degree.'

'You've moved around a bit.'

'Yes, I suppose we have.'

'Wasn't that unsettling for Holly?'

'She didn't seem to find it too difficult. She's always

made friends easily.' He put his hands in his pockets as they strolled on the rapidly cooling sand. A girl was running along the edge of the water with a large black dog, and a couple of teenagers in a dinghy fooled about a few yards out, but otherwise they had the beach to themselves. The tide had receded, and they were able to make their way around the big rock without having to wade. Here there was a steep cliff, and a mixture of sand and smooth, water-worn rock to walk on, and little pools holding waving seaweeds that hid scurrying, secretive sea-life.

They found a large, flat rock that was dry on top, and Drew climbed it and helped Karen to scramble up after him. Sitting side by side, they watched the sunset turn the water to a pale gold that faded into silver as the stars studded the sky one by one.

'Lovely, isn't it?' Karen said dreamily, resting her chin on her bent knees, her arms wrapped tightly about her shins.

'Mm, hmm.' Drew was sitting a little behind her, and when she turned her head she saw that he was looking at her with a strange, baffled and faintly angry expression.

She stirred nervously. 'Hadn't we better be getting back?' She got to her feet stiffly. She hadn't realised that they had been sitting there for so long. Drew seemed very big when he rose to his feet beside her, and she instinctively tried to put some distance between them, stepping back. There wasn't enough room, and she felt herself begin to fall, before Drew shot out a hand and hauled her close, her hand against his chest.

She snatched it away, but he didn't release her immediately. His hands spread against her back, he said drily, 'I'm not a mad rapist, you know. What are you scared of?' She felt the warmth of his chest against her breasts, and his breath stirred her hair.

'I'm not scared,' she said. 'Except of falling off this rock. I slipped, that's all.'

He held her a moment longer, then quite suddenly he freed her, jumped down and turned, offering her his hands. After a moment's pause, she put hers in them and jumped to the sand by his side while he steadied her. Darkness was descending fast, and he said, 'Come on. We'd better get round the rocks while we can still see.'

He touched her arm now and then to guide her, and once gave her his hand over a tricky spot, but after they regained the smooth sand he walked beside her with a foot of space between them, and when they reached the house, he didn't linger on the doorstep to savour the night, but opened the door for her and followed her in, switching on the centre light.

'I'll check on Holly,' he said. 'Will you put on the kettle?'

When he came back she was putting out two cups. The room seemed warm after the evening air, and a little stuffy. 'Coffee?' she asked him.

'Yes, thanks.'

When she had made it, he took his cup from her and leaned against the laminated vinyl bench while she carried hers to the table. The little Christmas tree had lost one of its tinsel streamers. She picked up the coil of silver and rearranged it among the branches. She remembered their first and last Christmas together when Holly was barely three months old. Karen had insisted on having a tree, a real pine tree, not a paper one from a shop, and Drew had gone out on Christmas Eve and driven for miles in the unreliable old car they had owned, to find one. It hadn't been much bigger than this, and it was lopsided, but they had decorated it together with what meagre trimmings they had been able to afford, and placed presents under it for Holly and for each other. And they had been happy. Drew's mother had come the next day for Christmas dinner, bringing a traditional plum pudding and gifts for all of them, and Karen had hoped that Mrs Bridger might be starting to forgive her for destroying her hopes for her son.

'What are you thinking about?' Drew asked softly, and she realised that her coffee was sitting untouched on the table in front of her.

'Nothing,' she answered hastily, and picked up the cup. Her eyes stung, and she quickly swallowed a couple of mouthfuls of hot liquid.

'Careful,' he said. 'You'll burn yourself.'

'It's not that hot.'

He came and sat opposite her. 'Then why are your eyes watering?'

She put down her cup. 'Do you have a hidden ambition to be a detective?'

He smiled and shook his head. 'What's wrong?'

She smiled back brightly. 'Nothing. I haven't had such a nice Christmas for ... a long time.'

'Since you left us, you mean?'

Her face closed, and he sighed impatiently. 'Wouldn't it be better to have it out in the open?'

'Is that why you asked me here?' she asked him.

'I asked you for Holly's sake,' he said sharply. 'And for yours. You looked as though you could do with a break.'

'You're not reponsible for me, Drew.'

'You don't need to remind me.' His voice was oddly harsh.

She glanced at him fleetingly, and then looked away. She picked up her cup again, and managed to drink the coffee, keeping her eyes on the table.

Drew suddenly put out his hand and clasped hers. 'Let's not fight,' he said. 'For Holly's sake. It's the season of goodwill. And it has been a good day, hasn't it? I don't want to spoil it.'

'Neither do I.'

'Good.' He lifted her hand and rubbed it against his cheek. It was a casual and yet curiously intimate gesture. 'More coffee?'

She shook her head, pushing the empty cup away. Drew stood up and took it with his to the sink and rinsed them.

Karen slid back her chair, yawning. 'I think I may sleep in tomorrow morning. Do you mind?'

'Feel free. Holly may wake you, banging about. She takes after me, an early riser. Not sleeping till all hours like you.'

'I don't sleep till all hours!'

'You used to, whenever you got the chance.'

'I used to be dead tired all the time,' she retorted. 'A baby cuts into one's sleep rather drastically.'

He raised his hands in a conciliatory gesture. 'OK, peace! Remember? And you can sleep as much as you want to, here. That's what holidays are for. Only if you're late for breakfast, you make your own, fair enough?'

'Fine. That's OK with me.' She was tempted to comment on his expertise in the kitchen, but that might fuel another argument. Obviously he had learned a lot of skills in the process of looking after Holly. She felt a familiar pang of guilt. But that was something she had lived with for a long, long time. 'I can cook, too,' she said carefully. 'I mean, if you want me to . . . any time, just ask.'

He put away the cups and came back to the table as she was getting up. 'Thanks,' he said. 'I may take you up on that.'

'Well,' she stood rather awkwardly, her hand on the chairback, 'I think I'll go to bed.'

'Sure. I'll try to keep the brat quiet for you in the morning.'

'Thank you. But Holly's not a brat. She's a nice child. You . . . you've done a good job,' she added painfully.

She had reached the bedroom door when he said softly, 'Karen?'

'Yes?' She paused with her hand on the knob.

He came slowly over to her and stood looking down into her wary eyes. 'Thank *you*,' he said softly. 'We haven't had such a wonderful Christmas for a long time, either. I'm glad you came.'

He put his hand to her cheek, touching it with his knuckles, and a flutter of alarm made her grasp his fingers. Then, somehow, they were twined in hers, and he was smiling at her, his eyes dark and unfathomable.

'Goodnight,' she said breathlessly, her fingers moving convulsively in his hold.

He laughed softly, and let her escape. 'Goodnight, Karen,' he said, and leaned over and opened the door for her.

CHAPTER SEVEN

THE BEACH was more crowded on Boxing Day. Karen, finding nobody about when she woke just before ten, made herself some toast and orange juice, and put on a pair of shorts, a cotton top and a light sweater before wandering down to the sand. She found Drew and Holly easily. Holly was climbing the rough branches of a pohutukawa that hung over the sand, and Drew was propped against its base, reading a book.

'Hi,' he said, as she came near. 'Enjoy your sleep?'

'Lovely, thank you.'

Holly called to her, and she tipped back her head and waved. The tree was old, and the branch Holly was clinging to swayed rather alarmingly. 'Is she all right up there?' Karen asked anxiously.

'Don't worry, she climbs like a cat. She's been climbing everything in sight since she was eighteen months old. Sit down.' He indicated the sand beside him, and moved over a little.

She said, 'Isn't that a bit young?'

'She was an early walker—barely eleven months. And she chattered nineteen to the dozen from the time she started talking.'

Karen looked down, her throat aching. She had missed all of that. 'How old was she then?' she asked.

'A bit more than a year.' He paused. 'I have photographs, if you'd like to see them some time.'

Photographs of Holly as a baby, a toddler, growing into a little girl, and then almost a teenager. 'Yes,' she said huskily. 'Yes, please, I'd like to see them.'

Holly had scrambled down the tree, and landed in a

shower of sand nearby. 'What are you talking about?' she asked.

'You,' Drew told her.

Intrigued, she asked, 'What were you saying?'

'Never mind.' He took pity and added, 'Karen wants to see your baby photos.'

'Those? Ooh, yuck! You won't show them to her, will you?'

Drew grinned, and Karen said, 'Please, Holly? I'd really like to see them.'

'We-ell. Promise not to laugh?'

'I won't laugh.'

'Anyway . . .' Holly said, and then stopped, her hands behind her back and her face red.

'What?' Karen asked.

'Well . . .' Then, with unwonted aggression, she burst out, 'Why weren't you *there*?'

Stunned, Karen sat silent. Holly looked down at the sand and said, 'You didn't have to go away.'

Karen scrambled to her knees, reaching for her daughter's hand. 'Yes, I *did*,' she said intensely. 'I know it's hard for you to understand, and I can't explain . . . at least, not just now. Maybe, when you're older. But it wasn't because I didn't love you, darling. Believe me. I loved you so much . . .' Her eyes swam with tears. 'I *did*,' she said passionately.

She swallowed, biting back the tears. Holly eyed her uncertainly. 'Why can't you explain now?' she demanded.

A horribly familiar, cold panic invaded Karen's body, bringing cold sweat to her temples. *Because I couldn't bear to have you know what I am . . . I couldn't bear to have you . . . and Drew . . . look at me with loathing . . . as you would if you knew . . .* A thousand remembered nightmares crowded her brain. 'I'm sorry.' She shook her head. 'I can't . . . not yet.'

Holly pulled her hand away, suddenly embarrassed.

'Daddy, can I go and climb up to the top of the cliff?'

'If you stick to the path.'

'Yeah, OK.' She wheeled and started off along the beach, and Karen sat back on her heels, watching her go.

'Well, it was a reasonable question,' Drew said drily.

She supposed it was. But it had been unexpected, coming out of the blue like that. Up until now, Holly had seemed to accept Karen's re-advent into her life with comparative ease, not questioning the past. Perhaps it wasn't going to be as easy as she had begun to think.

'Kids tend to blame themselves,' he said, 'when a parent leaves.'

She stared at him in horror. 'She doesn't . . . does she? You haven't let her think that it was her fault?'

'Of course I've tried not to. One doesn't always know what goes on in a child's mind.'

'She mustn't!' said Karen. 'She mustn't blame herself.'

'That's up to you,' he said cruelly. 'Only you can explain.'

Karen backed away, her face pale, fighting her emotions.

'Was there someone else?' Drew said abruptly.

'What?' She looked at him blankly.

'Was there another man? I wondered if you had a lover, when we were together. Did you go away with him?'

For a moment she very nearly burst into hysterical laughter. The idea was ludicrous. She and Drew had been married scarcely a year, and she had had Holly to look after, as well as trying to make a home out of a shabby old house which was all they could afford to rent. Apart from lacking temptation and opportunity, she hadn't had either the time or energy to be conducting a clandestine love affair. 'Of course I didn't!' she said. 'What a crazy idea!'

'It didn't seem so crazy to me,' he told her with some

irritation. 'Do you remember how often you'd had a "headache" or been "too tired" to make love, before you took off? It set me thinking.'

'That I'd been unfaithful to you?' Suddenly boiling with resentment, she stood up and said, 'Thanks a lot!'

She stalked off down the beach, making vaguely in the direction of the house, unfortunately impeded by the soft, yielding surface under her feet. She heard Drew's impatient exclamation and the subdued sound of his book hitting the sand before he came after her.

'I take it I was wrong,' he said as he came up with her.

Throwing him a furious glance, she said, 'If I said I had a headache, I had a *headache*. If I said I was tired, it was because I'd spent the best part of the previous twenty-four hours, and the twenty-four hours before that, and before that, looking after your child, and keeping your house, and doing your washing and ironing, and shopping for your food and cooking your meals! I might have taken a lover, if I hadn't been too damned busy! And anyway, who would have wanted me? I looked like a wet dishrag!'

'Rubbish!'

'Well, I certainly felt like one!'

'If you were overworked . . .'

'*If . . .!*' she said derisively. A resentment that she had bottled up at the time filled the single word with a world of meaning. 'My God, that's an understatement.' She had never even realised then just how tired she had been. Walking round in a fog of exhaustion had become normal for her.

His brows knitted in perplexity. 'You never complained about it then,' he pointed out, his hand running over his hair. 'You know I'd have helped out, if you'd asked.'

'How could I?' she snapped. 'You were never there to complain to. You had your career, and your university courses, and every night that you weren't out attending lectures, you were buried in books and papers.'

'You wanted me to go on with my studies!' he reminded her. 'We both knew that things would be rough for a year or two, but we'd decided that in the long run it would be worth it. It was going to mean a better life for all of us in the end. I thought you were keen for me to get my degree.'

'I *was*! Only I didn't realise what it would be like. It sounded fine, before the baby arrived. I thought I could cope with a house and a husband and a baby. But I was only eighteen, and it was all so new to me ...'

'My mother was always willing to help. You know that. She would have stepped in any time.'

In the middle of the night, when the baby wanted a feed? Karen asked herself ironically. But that was hardly fair. Certainly at any time of the day Drew's mother would have been only too eager to come and help. She was frighteningly efficient at things like getting nappies snow white and removing brown rings from the bath, and serving a balanced meal every evening that had been properly planned the day before. She had never needed to thaw the meat an hour before it was due on the table, or found that she had no greens in the house to put in the pot. And she was full of good advice about housekeeping, cooking and child rearing. When she 'popped in to see how the baby's doing' two or three times a week, if Holly was screaming while Karen tried unsuccessfully to soothe her, Mrs Bridger would expertly remove the baby from her mother's arms, and have her cooing within minutes.

'There,' she would say to Karen. 'Just hold her firmly like this, on your shoulder, and rub her back, see? She'll soon bring up that nasty wind.' Or, 'Try massaging her gums, dear. Like this.' And Karen would try, and the baby would wriggle and grimace and end up screaming again. And Mrs Bridger, suppressing a sigh, would take over and do everything necessary until Holly fell asleep and could be put into her cot again.

How, Karen thought now, could she possibly explain
to Drew that his mother's best intentions had merely
made her feel hopelessly inadequate? Once she had got
over her initial horror that Drew was proposing to throw
in his full-time university course to marry Karen, she
had been a wonderful mother-in-law. She had never
criticised Karen for her inexperienced cooking, her
muddled housekeeping or her deficiencies as a mother,
but had kept her rather obvious thoughts to herself. She
had done her best to remedy the gaps in Karen's
education, pressing on her simple if time-consuming
recipes for cheap, nourishing meals, recommending
good old-fashioned home-made cleaning methods to
save money on expensive commercial products, and
patiently correcting the mistakes Karen made in
babycare. It wasn't her fault that her daughter-in-law
had come to see her helpful visits as a form of
supervision, and 'popping in to see how the baby's
doing' as an excuse to rescue Holly from Karen's
incompetent mothering.

'Your mother was very good to me,' she mumbled
resignedly.

'Yes.' Feelingly, he added, 'I only wish I'd had her
help when I had to look after Holly myself.'

Do you? Karen thought grimly. She pulled herself up.
He would have welcomed it, of course. Not seen it, as she
inevitably and unfairly had, as interference, not wanted
to scream with frustration every time Mrs Bridger,
flushed at completing yet another demonstration of how
to go about some minor household task, stood back and
said, 'There, dear, now isn't it easier that way? Next
time you'll know . . .'

Someone called Drew's name, and he turned his head.
Coming along the beach towards them were a man and a
woman, their arms linked. The man was tall and
muscular, with curly sand-coloured hair, and wearing

denim cut-offs, and the woman was a slim, pretty brunette in bikini top and cotton pants. 'Hello, Sandy,' Drew said as they came near. 'Suzie—how are you? Have you just arrived?'

'Twenty minutes ago,' Sandy told him, glancing at his watch. 'The kids couldn't wait to get down to the beach.'

Drew said, 'This is Karen—Sandy and Suzie Harding. They have the green house with the striped awnings on the windows.'

Karen remembered it. It was one of a cluster about fifty yards from Drew's.

Sandy engulfed Karen's hand in his, and cocked an enquiring brow at Drew, who ignored it. Suzie looked interested, but confined herself to a smile as she said warmly, 'Hello, Karen.'

'Hello,' Karen answered a bit stiffly. What Sandy was thinking, as he grinned broadly at Drew, was rather obvious.

Two children, a boy and a girl, scampered up to the group bearing a trail of seaweed each, and were introduced as Jason and Katrina.

'Where's Holly?' Katrina wanted to know.

'She went up the cliff,' Drew answered, and, scarcely pausing to get permission from their parents, the two children went off to join her.

'Hey!' Sandy roared after them. 'Your mother and I are going back to the house soon. You come home by twelve, or you'll get no lunch.'

They waved and made for the cliff path. Suzie turned to Drew and said, 'Why don't you and Karen come with us, and we'll have a quiet drink while the kids are occupied? They'll be all right, keeping an eye on one another.'

Drew seemed to hesitate. Then he said, 'Thanks. OK, Karen?'

'Yes, of course.' As they turned to accompany the

other two, Karen said, 'You've forgotten your book.'

He went back to fetch it, and as they walked slowly, waiting for him to catch up, Suzie said to Karen, 'Holly and our two are great mates. They only see each other in school holidays, but they just seem to pick up where they left off.'

'Holly will be glad to see them,' Karen said, pushing down an absurd sense of jealousy. The Hardings weren't an intrusion. They were part of Holly and Drew's lives, and of course Holly would want to spend some time with her friends. Drew, too.

He came up with them, holding the book, and Suzie said, 'What are you reading?'

It turned out that she had read it, too, and they discussed the plot and characters while Sandy came to walk beside Karen, regarding her with scarcely veiled curiosity. 'Do you come from Auckland, Karen?'

'Yes. Not originally, but I've been living there for ten years now.'

'Known Drew long?'

'I knew him a long time ago,' she said carefully. 'We just met again recently.' She supposed Holly might cause a sensation by mentioning the relationship, no one had sworn her to secrecy. But Drew obviously hadn't previously mentioned her name to these friends of his, and he hadn't offered to explain. She didn't want to explain either. It had been rather disconcerting to find that there was a community of people here who knew Drew and his daughter. She had assumed that the house was just rented for this year's holiday, and that they would be an anonymous family among other holiday-makers who had never met before, and who wouldn't see one another again.

The children arrived back at five minutes past twelve, while the adults were still sitting and talking on the timber deck on the front of the Hardings' house. Suzie and Karen had found a mutual interest in romantic-thriller novels, and were getting on well while Drew listened to Sandy's plans for spending a good part of his holiday fishing. A smartly painted boat with an outboard motor sat on a trailer on the patchy buffalo grass that passed for a lawn, and several rods were still tied to a rack on top of the estate car parked beside the house.

'Oh, heck!' Suzie said with mock disgust as the children thudded on to the decking in their bare, sand-crusted feet. 'I suppose I'll have to set about finding something to feed them on.'

'Why don't they come over to our place for lunch?' Drew suggested, getting to his feet. 'You and Sandy can finish unpacking in peace, then.'

'Oh, Drew, you angel! Would you mind, Karen?'

'Of course not.'

Katrina and Jason were saying eagerly, 'Can we, Mum?' And Holly put in a request for chips and tomato sauce.

Karen helped Drew to prepare them, and they added a couple of saveloys each to the pan and let the children take their plates outside to sit on the steps.

Sitting at the table with Drew, Karen said quietly, 'The Hardings don't know who I am, do they?'

'They're only holiday acquaintances. I've never mentioned you.'

'Supposing Holly says something?'

His brows rose. 'It's not a deep, dark secret, is it? Will it matter?'

'No, but you ... didn't say anything when you introduced us.'

'It didn't seem worth going into all the explanations. And I didn't think that you'd want me to.'

'I don't. But ... they're going to wonder.'

'Let them,' he said carelessly. 'It's none of their business, and they're not the nosey kind.'

'They're curious, though.'

He looked suddenly amused. 'Does it bother you? Do

you want me to tell them that we're legally married, and the proprieties are not being violated?'

'No, of course not. I don't suppose they're that interested, anyway.'

'Probably not.'

'Daddy, are there any more chips?' Holly had got up from the step and come into the room.

'On the bench. What about the others?'

'I'll take the dish outside.'

Watching them empty the dish on to their plates, Karen said bemusedly, 'Where on earth do they put it all?'

'They're all hollow right through at that age,' Drew grinned. 'You have a lot to learn.'

She glanced at him warily, but there was nothing but humour in his face.

Drew suggested the children wash up, and they did it with good grace. Karen watched him talking to them, and envied the casualness of his friendly but firm manner. One thing about having children around, she reflected, it successfully prevented the tension between herself and Drew from building up to unbearable proportions.

She found that it was useful to have the Hardings about, too. She liked Suzie and Sandy, and their children were pleasant and polite, and clearly added a good deal to Holly's enjoyment of her holiday. Sometimes other children were about as well, and Karen was introduced to a couple of families who were regular visitors to the place, and once or twice exchanged a few words with some who were staying for the first time. It was a small community, and those who had houses soon came to know one another, at least by sight.

'Those kids are having a wonderful time,' Suzie commented to Karen one day as they lay on the beach and watched her two and Holly playing about in the shallows with an old inner tube. 'Pity Holly doesn't have brothers or sisters.'

Karen supposed that was true, and felt a pang of guilt. She shot a quick look at Suzie and decided that the remark had been quite unconscious. Evidently Holly had said nothing about Karen being her mother. Since Christmas Day Holly had reverted to addressing her by her name. Karen told herself it didn't matter, and it certainly didn't mean anything. But with that uncharacteristic outburst niggling at the edge of her mind, she couldn't help wondering if her daughter was hiding some resentment and anger against her.

Drew had yielded to an invitation from Sandy to go fishing, and later that day Karen and Holly went strolling alone on the beach, picking up shells and putting them into a plastic bag. 'What are you going to do with them?' Holly asked, as she carefully placed a tiny, pink, fan-shaped scallop into the bag.

'I'm developing a new line of pale pink satin underthings,' Karen said. 'I think I'll call it "seashell" and have a window display with some sand and a few shells arranged around the clothing.'

'Sounds nice,' Holly commented. 'Can I help?'

'Yes, if you like. The bag is almost full. Shall we sit down for a while before we walk back?'

They went up on to dry sand, and sat propped against an old weathered trunk of driftwood. Holly bent her knees and dug her toes into the sand, and Karen tipped back her head to enjoy the sun on her face.

After a while Holly said, 'I s'pose I should have known who you were the minute I saw you. It was a bit dumb not recognising my own mother, wasn't it?'

'It wasn't dumb!' Karen said, taken aback. 'How could you be expected to?'

'Daddy had some photos. But you've changed a lot, haven't you? And they weren't very good ones, really. I liked you, though. D'you think deep down, I really did know who you were?'

'I don't know. I ... hope so, Holly.'

'Did you know who *I* was?'

'Yes.'

Holly turned to her, and Karen was tempted for a moment to let the child believe that she had experienced some kind of psychic recognition. But she said, 'Because you were with your father.'

'Oh, yes. He wanted you to see me. He said so afterwards ... you know, when he told me that you were my mother.'

'Did he?' Karen wondered if he had given Holly any inkling of his motives. 'Did he say why?'

Holly's smooth forehead wrinkled. 'Not really. Just that you were my mother, and he thought you should see me.' She paused. 'It's kind of funny, having a mother after all this time. I mean, it's nice, but it's ... funny. Kind of ... hard to get used to. I keep thinking that one morning I'll wake up and you'll be gone again.'

Karen's throat ached as she looked down at Holly's face, half turned away from her, the untidy ponytail losing strands of fine pale hair as usual. 'I'll try not to let that happen,' she promised huskily. Cautiously she added, 'It wasn't your fault, you know, that I went away. I hope you didn't think it was.'

There was a short pause.

'The thing is,' Holly said, 'it's sort of hard to believe that you really *are* my mother.'

'Is that why you haven't told Jason and Katrina?'

Holly looked up. 'Oh, I did tell them! The very first day they were here. They thought I was making it up. Katrina said you were too young to be my mother, anyway. Well, you *look* too young.'

Yes, I was, Karen thought, far too young. If I'd been older, perhaps I might have coped better than I did ...

Holly said, 'Katrina's mother's quite young, isn't she? But not as young as you. There's a girl in my class at school, and *her* mother's got grey hair!'

Karen smiled. 'I guess mothers can be quite young or quite old.'

'What was *your* mother like?'

'I . . . don't remember her very well. She . . .' About to say, 'She died when I was small,' as she always had when asked about her parentage, Karen hesitated, recalling Drew's injunction not to lie to Holly. Surely it wouldn't matter? But she had promised to obey him, and she said carefully, 'She wasn't able to look after me properly, and when I was four I went to live with some other people.'

'Why couldn't she look after you?' Holly asked, curiously. 'Was she sick?'

And Karen cravenly answered, 'Yes.' Wrapping her arms about her, she fingered one of the small, faded scars on her shoulder. 'She was sick,' she repeated. *My mother did this,* she could have said. *And those scars on my thigh, my mother did that, too. My mother was a monster. I was taken away from her for my own safety.*

But surely even Drew didn't demand that much truth.

'Did she die?'

'Yes,' Karen said eventually. Her uncle had said so. She wanted to believe it. Her uncle had seldom lied.

'What about your father? Couldn't he have looked after you instead?'

Karen shook her head. 'My father went away when I was just a baby.'

'Like you?' Holly asked.

Karen flushed. 'I suppose so,' she said. 'Yes.' *But I had a better reason. A compelling, inescapable reason.*

'I'm glad Daddy didn't get sick. Who would have looked after me, then?'

'I thought . . . your grandmother would have. Daddy's mother. She loved you, and I asked her . . . hoped she'd take my place.' *I didn't just abandon you,* she wanted to say. *I tried to make sure you would be well looked after, cared for much better than I could do it.* 'But she died.'

'Yes, I know. There's a picture of her in Daddy's room. He told me about her. My grandad, too. But he died when Daddy was sixteen.'

'Yes.' Drew had spoken of his father quite a lot in the early days. Karen had liked to listen, never having known her own father. He and Drew seemed to have had a good relationship, and the suddenness of his death from an unsuspected heart defect had made the loss more traumatic for his teenage son. Perhaps it was one reason why, at twenty, he had seemed to Karen more mature than most of the young men she had met.

'Did you have a grandmother and grandfather?' Holly asked.

'My mother's parents died before I was born. I don't know anything about my father's family.' Holly's great-grandparents. How remote that seemed. On her side, the family tree was sadly lacking in continuity. Drew's had much more stability. *Until he married me,* she thought. *Until I left him.*

'People die an awful lot, don't they?'

'Older people do,' Karen agreed, wondering if the conversation was getting morbid, and not eager to prolong it, anyway. 'Come on, let's get back. If those men don't catch any fish, we'll have to find something to eat in the cupboards.'

There was, after all, fresh fish for tea, and some more to be placed in the smoker at the rear of the Hardings' house. While Drew went over to help Sandy set up the smoker and prepare the fish for it, Karen and Holly dredged fillets of snapper in egg and breadcrumbs.

'Aunty Maggie used to do them in batter, just like the fish and chip shop,' Holly said.

'Aunty Maggie?' Drew had been an only child. It was one of the things they had delighted in having in common, when they first met. 'Who's she?'

'She used to live with us, but then she got married.

She made yummy chocolate cake, too. And fudge! And nut toffee. She taught me to make it.'

A housekeeper, Karen surmised. Of course Drew must have had someone to help when he went back to work again. Aunty Maggie sounded like a homely, motherly sort of person. She was probably a whizz at removing dirt rings from baths, too. 'I'm not much good at batter,' Karen said. 'Mine sort of slides off the fish, and it leaves little burnt blobs floating round in the oil.'

Holly giggled. 'Never mind,' she said. 'I like breadcrumbs, too. Have we got any lemons?'

'I saw some in the fridge. Your father seems to think of everything.' His mother and Aunty Maggie had set him a good example. 'You can cut them into wedges, if you like.'

When Drew came in again, he said to Holly, 'Jason and Katrina are going out in the boat with their parents tomorrow. You're invited, chicken.'

'Great! I can go, can't I, Daddy?'

He tweaked her hair. 'Sure, if you behave yourself and do just as Mr Harding tells you. And never take off your life-jacket.'

'I know, I know. Bet I catch more fish than you!'

Drew laughed. 'That's a bit rash. I'm not sure if there's going to be much fishing, anyway. I think it's more of a family picnic. Mrs Harding isn't all that keen on fishing. They said something about anchoring at an island.'

'Neat!' Holly said. 'A real island!'

Karen smiled. 'I always used to dream of having an island to myself, when I was about your age.'

Drew looked at her. 'No man is an island,' he quoted. 'Nor woman, either.'

'Still,' Karen argued, 'it was a nice dream.'

It had been an escape route, if an inadequate one. At eleven she had not been particularly happy. Her Uncle George—her great-uncle really, her grandfather's brother—had taken her into his household, after she had spent some time in social welfare homes. His charity arose chiefly from a sense of duty and perhaps even more a feeling of shame that any family member should be a charge on the welfare state. There he felt his obligation to her was more than adequately fulfilled, and the actual care of the child had devolved on his wife, Ada. With her own family growing up and virtually off her hands, Aunt Ada had looked forward to being free to spend the days on the golf course or at the bridge table, but instead was saddled with a six-year-old girl to look after. It was not a prospect she enjoyed, and she spent the next ten years in a state of perpetual martyrdom.

At first Karen had shared a room with their teenage daughter, and Brenda, accustomed to privacy, had resented her presence bitterly. The three older brothers had simply ignored the little girl, who tried her best to keep out of their way. When she reached puberty, they found it fun to tease her, but by then they were not living at home, and she only had to endure the embarrassment of their uncomfortable masculine presence when they visited their parents on the odd weekend.

Materially, Karen had wanted for nothing. Uncle George was a respected lawyer with a very good income, and Aunt Ada, admitting that 'at least the child pays for dressing' had never grudged spending money on clothes for her. She was certainly no Cinderella. Aunt Ada didn't even expect her to help in the house. Apart from making her own bed and keeping her room neat, Karen had few chores. Aunt Ada liked to cook, and Karen's fumbling efforts to help in the kitchen were more often than not spurned. She learned the rudiments, but Aunt Ada couldn't be bothered spending time teaching her the finer points, and didn't like her trying her hand alone and 'making a mess of my oven and using my things'. A woman came twice a week to cope with the heavier work and do the washing, so there were few ways in which an inefficient schoolgirl could make herself useful.

She often told herself she was ungrateful, knowing that she was fortunate in living in a beautiful home, having a wardrobe of smart clothes, and being provided with more than adequate food and not only the necessities but the luxuries of life. She should have been very happy. Certainly her relatives seemed to assume that she was. It was no doubt her own fault that in spite of all that, in spite, even, of expensive Christmas and birthday presents which were punctiliously given to her on the appropriate occasions, she had always felt like an outsider.

CHAPTER EIGHT

KAREN felt restless that evening. After Holly had gone to bed, she went to stand in the doorway, watching the low breakers pushing at the shore. The day had been hot, and the evening was still and warm. A couple of children scampered along the beach with a dog, a man walking more slowly behind them. The dog was yelping and jumping, and every now and then it twisted its head and body to see if its human playmates were keeping up. Karen realised it was the same animal she had seen before with a young girl in tow.

'Did Holly ever have a dog?' she asked Drew, without turning her head. Drew got up from the sofa where he had been leafing through a magazine. 'No,' he said, coming over to her, leaning against the door frame with his hands in the pockets of his jeans. 'She had a cat for a couple of years, but it got killed by a car. She said she didn't want another one.'

'Oh, poor Holly!'

'She got over it.'

She thought he sounded callous, and looked up at him indignantly.

'Kids get over most things,' he said, his voice taking on a slight edge. 'Fortunately.'

She was in no position to throw stones, of course. Biting her lip, she turned her head away, staring blindly at the rapidly darkening seascape.

Drew gave a sharp sigh. He stirred and took his hands from his pockets, seeming to hesitate. 'Why don't we go for a walk? It's a glorious evening, and we only have two more days.'

She had tried not to think about that. The holiday had gone too swiftly. Tomorrow Holly would be away for most of the day, and the next would be their last. After lunch they would have to pack and go.

'All right,' she said.

'Will you need a jacket or something?'

Karen shook her head. She was wearing a denim skirt and a peach-coloured, loose textured-cotton top with roomy push-up sleeves. 'I'll be warm enough.'

'Come on, then.' He put his hand at her waist as they went down the steps to the sandy ground, then she waited while he turned back to close the door behind them, cutting off the shaft of light from the house.

The sudden darkness was disconcerting, but in a few minutes the moonlight proved to be bright enough to see by. The sand glimmered whitely, and creamy waves slid with a sibilant whisper up the gentle slope, eddying round their bare feet as they reached the water's edge and turned to walk along the curved length of the beach.

Drew's arm came about her, holding her firmly to his side, and she didn't resist. It felt good. They walked in silence until stopped by the jutting headland that marked the end of the beach. They stood in the shadow of its pale, sheer bluff, not very high but difficult to climb, with scattered flax and scrubby, dry-leaved manuka bushes at the top. Karen turned to go back, and Drew's arm slipped from her shoulder. He caught at her hand, and then the other one, so that she had to face him in the twilight. She couldn't see his expression, only his eyes were a brief glitter in the dimly seen mask of his face, and when he spoke she saw a glimpse of his white teeth. 'Wait,' he said.

She stood expectantly, half in hope and half in trepidation. She wasn't sure what she wanted of this encounter, nor what Drew might want of her.

'You look so young,' he said quietly. 'Watching you with Holly, sometimes you don't seem much older than she does . . . especially when you do your hair like that.' He lifted a hand to touch the ponytail, and his thumb brushed her nape. His fingers found the elastic tie that had already slipped a little, and he slid it further until it came off and her hair spread across her shoulders. 'That's better,' he said. 'At least you don't look quite such a child.'

'Drew ...' She moved her head a little, a token effort to pull away from his hand as it threaded through her hair.

'Shh,' he said, and placed a finger on her lips with a gentle pressure. Then the pressure eased, but he was stroking her mouth with his finger, back and forth in a light, erotic touch, and his other hand travelled from her hair down her back to her waist, pulling her to him.

His finger left her lips, and his hand strayed across her cheek, brushing back a strand of hair, slipping under it to curve about her nape.

'Drew ...' she whispered. 'I don't know that this is a good idea.'

He tugged gently at her hair, tipping back her head. 'Why not?' he murmured, his lips just touching hers and then lifting a fraction, going to her cheek, and caressing her neck, then returning to tantalise her mouth, his breath warm on her lips as he whispered, 'You want it, don't you?'

She felt herself begin to tremble, her mouth softening and parting even as she moaned, 'No, I ...'

'*Liar*.' He took her mouth properly this time, his lips hard and compelling, making her accept him, making her respond.

She was going up in flames, her blood on fire. When his arms tightened about her she pressed herself against him, and felt the answering throb and thrust of his desire. She swayed on her feet, and he released her mouth and buried his lips in the curve of her neck and shoulder. He shifted his stance so that he stood with his legs apart, supporting her, and his mouth went to the hollow at the base of her throat, his tongue probing the accelerated pulse that beat there.

She clung to him, dizzy and hot and drenched in

passion. Her loose top rode up under his hands, and he
pushed them under the fabric to touch her skin, his
fingers finding the pliant groove of her spine, than
exploring her ribcage and the curve of her breast. As his
palm closed firmly over it, she gasped, and his mouth
took hers again with blatant sensuality. Fireworks were
exploding in her brain, his mouth and his hands sending
waves of pleasure rippling through her.

He suddenly broke the kiss, still holding her, and said,
with his cheek against hers, his voice unsteady, 'Let's go
back to the house.'

She swallowed and nodded. He kissed her forehead
and her eyelids and turned her with his arm hard about
her waist towards the house. Once he stopped to pull her
into his arms again and kiss her deeply, but her response
was less headlong than before. He held her away, trying
to see her face. 'Something wrong?'

Karen shook her head, quite unable to reply. But as
they neared the house, she was aware of a growing sense
of unease. The mindless wanting began to recede, and
caution took over. She had never intended anything like
this. She didn't think that Drew had, either. A long time
ago she had learned that the results of a few moments'
impulsive passion could lead to consequences both
unforeseen and irreversible. She had for many years
been in control of her life and her emotions. Never
again, she had vowed, would sexual desire override her
rational thought processes. She had determined to be
strong. And it had worked, until now. It didn't make any
difference that Drew was legally still her husband. If she
allowed the lovemaking he had begun to go its full
course, their relationship would have drastically altered,
entered a completely new phase. She wasn't at all sure
what he wanted from it, and she was even less certain of
her own feelings, apart from a wholly blind and
alarmingly physical need of the moment.

When he opened the door, the light was still on, and
she blinked in its sudden cruel glare. Drew closed the

door behind them, locking it with a distinct click of the key, and she stepped away from him, so that his embracing arm fell to his side.

Karen began to walk towards the kitchen area. Huskily she said, 'Do you want coffee?'

He was right behind her, his arms going about her to bring her back against him. 'No. I want to go to bed.' His lips nuzzled at the skin just below her ear. 'Come with me, darling.'

With an effort of will as well as strength, she put her hands on his wrists and pulled them away, shaking her head. 'No,' she said. He said something under his breath and with his hand on her arm pulled her round; then, as she resisted, hauled her into his arms and kissed her properly, his arms locked about her, his mouth forcing hers open, fiercely invasive. Waves of desire beat over her, and she almost gave in, but she managed to stiffen her body, to wrench away her head at last and say again, 'No, Drew! Stop!'

He let her go, his eyes incredulous, and stood staring at her.

Karen stepped back, her legs unsteady. 'I'm . . . sorry.'

There was a long silence. She avoided his eyes, her head down, a hand going nervously to her hair, tucking it back behind her ear.

'I don't understand,' he said, finally. 'Did I misinterpret the signals?'

'Yes,' she said, then, 'no. Not really. But I . . . wasn't thinking.'

'It isn't a prerequisite,' he said drily. Then, advancing on her, 'Maybe I should just stop you doing it for a while.'

She tried to stave him off, but she was no match for his strength. He captured her and laughed down at her flushed, angry face.

'Don't!' she said in stifled tones. 'It won't do any good, Drew.'

'Relax. I promise you'll enjoy it.'

'You mean you'll make me enjoy it?' she enquired coolly.

'Do you think I couldn't?' There was challenge in his voice, in his glittering eyes.

'But I don't want you to ... Look where not thinking got us last time.'

His eyes narrowed, then he abruptly let her go. 'It got us Holly,' he said. 'Are you sorry about that?'

'No, of course I'm not sorry for ... creating her. That's the good part. The rest ...'

He frowned as she made a futile, helpless gesture with her hand and shook her head. 'Was the rest so bad?' he asked harshly.

'No girl likes to be married because she's pregnant.'

'All right. We got off to a bad start. I seduced you, and I guess that makes me all kinds of a bastard. Hell, I *know* it does. I have no excuses, except ... I was still pretty young, myself.'

She looked at him at last, and said, 'I wasn't exactly an unwilling party.' A wry smile touching her lips, she added, 'Your mother was fairly obviously of the opinion that I'd seduced *you*!'

Reluctantly, Drew smiled too. 'Let's agree that we seduced each other,' he suggested. 'We always did find it pretty difficult to exercise much self-control when we were together. I should at least have made sure you didn't get pregnant, though.'

'It was as much my fault ... and maybe if I hadn't been trying to pretend that it wasn't happening ... if I hadn't been too shy to go to a doctor or a clinic ...'

Drew shrugged. 'There's no point in apportioning blame, now.'

'No. But I don't want to get into a similar situation, ever again. I've taken control of my life, and I like it that way. I like to think things through before I commit myself to anything.'

'That's a pretty bleak way to conduct a relationship, isn't it?'

'It could save a lot of heartbreak.'

'You never do anything on impulse ... never follow your feelings?'

'Not if I can help it.' That was one reason why she had found the meeting with him, and Holly's advent, so unsettling. Her painstakingly achieved, unemotional lifestyle had been knocked awry.

'You must miss out on a lot of fun.'

'*Fun* has to be paid for,' she reminded him tartly.

He inclined his head. 'OK. I take your point.'

'Good,' she said, 'fine. Now ... do you mind if I go to bed?'

'Alone, one presumes.'

'That's right.'

He stood blocking her way, looking down at her speculatively, and her heart skipped a beat or two. If he tried again, she wasn't sure if she would be strong enough to resist. She could see that he was weighing the temptation. She swallowed, her eyes unconsciously pleading, and said, her voice low, 'Please, Drew.'

He stood aside, but as she passed, caught her arm. She was still half turned from him, stubbornly keeping her face averted, but he tugged at her arm until he could lean down and touch her mouth with his. It was a brief kiss, but not gentle, his exasperation showing. Chillingly, she thought there was something calculated about it. Then he released her abruptly and said, 'Goodnight, Karen.'

Holly went off, sparkling with anticipation, early the next morning. Realising that she and Drew would be alone for the rest of the day, Karen tried to banish the events of the previous evening from her mind, and to treat him with cool indifference. His manner to her was casual, and she wasn't sure if she was imagining things when she detected a watchful look in his eyes.

After breakfast she said, 'I'm going to wash my hair. It needs a proper conditioning treatment after all the salt water and sun. Will you be wanting the bathroom for the next hour or so?'

'No. Be my guest. I'll stroll down to the beach, I think. I feel lazy today.'

It had really been an excuse, and the whole exercise was quite pointless, when she had every intention of swimming again later in the day, but she took her time over her hair, even sitting on the step afterwards and brushing it nearly dry in the sun. But it was still barely ten o'clock when she plaited it and pinned it firmly in a high knot on her head. She applied a light make-up and smoothed sunscreen all over her body before donning a bright red bikini and tying a light cotton sarong about her waist. Then she picked up a large beach towel and the library book she had not yet finished, and made her way slowly to the beach.

She couldn't avoid seeing Drew. He had chosen a spot almost directly in front the house, near one of the trees but outside the pool of shade it cast on the sand. Wearing only his swimming trunks, he was sitting on a light rug and his book lay face down beside him. She was relieved to see that he was not alone. Talking to him were a middle-aged couple whom she remembered being briefly introduced to some days ago. They had two grown sons who most days rode off up the steep road away from the beach on noisy motorbikes, sometimes spending their time roaring around on the hills behind the beach, or horseplaying on the sand for the benefit of any teenage girls who happened to be about. The parents had been quite pleasant to talk to, and their names, she remembered with a slight effort, were Carol and Leo, but she couldn't recall their surname.

At least she managed to greet them by their first names, as she came near. They seemed pleased to see her, and she stood talking to them for a few minutes, but soon they went off along the beach, calling, 'See you tonight, you two!'

Karen looked an enquiry at Drew, and he said,

'They've invited us to a New Year's Eve barbecue tonight. The boys have asked some of their friends over from Whangarei, and I think Carol and Leo would like some moral support. I said we'd probably be there.'

'Sounds fun,' Karen commented. New Year's Eve, and their last day here. A celebration seemed called for.

'You don't have to give it some thought before accepting the invitation?' he asked. Then, as she looked at him, 'I withdraw that. Forget it. Aren't you going to sit down?' He moved over on the rug, making room for her, and Karen hesitated. Not accepting the tacit invitation would seem like a calculated snub, after that remark, and she didn't want to look as though she was holding a grudge over a bit of minor and immediately retracted snideness. She didn't blame him for being a bit fed up over last night. She still hadn't quite regained her own equilibrium, and it must have smarted with him to be rejected after her initial admittedly eager co-operation.

In the end she sat down next to him, and rather stiffly remained upright with her arms wrapped about her knees, while he lounged beside her on one elbow. 'I hope Holly's enjoying herself,' she said, casting about for a safe topic.

'She will be. Meantime, why don't you relax and do the same?'

'I'm quite relaxed.'

'You don't look it. You're as nervous as a cat. Come on, I won't bite.'

Annoyed that he had noticed her tension, she took a deep breath and made a conscious effort to let go. Her head dipped on to her knees for a moment, and then she slowly let her hands fall, and lay back on the rug.

'Better?' she asked him, with gentle mockery.

His eyes ran over her with blatant appreciation, making her tense again. 'Mm. Got some sunscreen?'

'I'm smothered in it.'

'Pity.'

'Do you want me to get burnt?'

'I was hoping I'd be able to put it on for you.'

Her lashes swept down over her eyes. 'Don't . . . flirt with me, Drew.'

'Why not? Is there a law against a man flirting with his own wife?'

She cast him a fleeting glance. 'I'm not——'

'Yes, you are. I've got the bit of paper to prove it.'

'The bit of paper doesn't mean much, does it?'

'It means a lot to me, Karen. It always did. I can't answer for what it ever meant to you . . . if anything.'

'That's not fair!' She sat up, flushing. 'It did mean something to me!'

'Past tense?' he rapped.

She looked away again, closing her eyes as her teeth clenched on a sigh. There was a short, sharp silence.

'All right,' he said. 'Let's drop the subject.'

He picked up his book and turned over on his stomach, riffling pages rather ostentatiously. Karen debated whether to get up and go for a walk and calm down, but it seemed unnecessarily melodramatic, and she reached for her sunglasses and her own book, and began to read.

At first she had to reread every paragraph, forcing herself to concentrate, but after a while the sun and the ocean's song soothed her frayed nerves, and she became absorbed in the story. When Drew stood up and said, 'I'm going for a swim—coming?' she realised that she was hot, her thighs burning, and damp patches of sweat under her arms, between her breasts and at the backs of her knees.

'Yes,' she said, sitting up and removing her glasses.

Drew pulled her to her feet, and his smile was almost friendly. 'Come on.' He tugged at her hand, and they ran down the beach to the water and plunged in.

Surfacing, Karen shook the water from her eyes and said, 'Uugh!' The first shock was cold, but Drew merely laughed and called her a 'sook' and said the water was perfect. She made a face at him and swam away, within a few minutes admitting that he was right. The water was lovely, and it was quite a long time before she wanted to get out.

She patted her face dry with the towel, and gave her front a cursory drying before lying prone on the rug to allow the sun to complete the process. Drew flopped down beside her, saying, 'That hairstyle is remarkably durable. It seems to have stayed in place.'

'It was meant to. It has a dozen pins in it.'

He grinned and turned over on his back, an arm cradling his head. 'So if I get out of line, I'm likely to get skewered by a hairpin?'

'Possibly,' she said, checking with her fingers that they were all in place.

'I'll watch my step.' As she lowered her hand, he reached out and caught it in his. 'Let's call a truce,' he suggested.

'I thought we'd done that when we arrived here,' she answered. His fingers were warm on hers, and she didn't try to escape his clasp.

'Well,' he said softly, 'maybe I want more than a truce.'

She looked at him warily, and he tightened his fingers and said, 'I might want to start all over again, for instance.'

'For instance?'

His eyes were on their linked hands. 'Last night, I guess you felt you were being rushed into something you weren't ready for. But ... I still want you, Karen. And last night you wanted me, that much was obvious, until you had second thoughts. Let's lay it on the line. I won't push too hard, and you stop trying to freeze me off ... and maybe something will work out.'

What sort of something, she wondered. 'What ... exactly are you thinking of?'

He moved restlessly. 'Must you have everything cut and dried? I can't make you any promises. But I think we could have ... a relationship that works.'

'Supposing it doesn't?'

'You could at least give it a chance. It could be good. Karen ... believe me. It could be the best thing that's ever happened, for either of us ... and for Holly.'

He wasn't asking for much, she realised. He hadn't suggested that they might renew their marriage, but if she lowered the barriers she had built, anything might happen. The thought was frightening ... and persuasive. Perhaps he was right. She ought to give it a chance.

'All right,' she said slowly. 'I won't freeze you ... but that doesn't mean,' she added hastily, 'that I'll sleep with you.'

'I know.' He grinned, and leaned over and kissed her cheek. 'Good girl,' he said, in the same tone he would have used to Holly. Then he lay back on the rug and closed his eyes with the air of a man who had accomplished something.

Karen realised that it was ridiculous to feel piqued. She looked down at his tanned face, the straight brows, the closed eyes and the slight, satisfied curve of his mouth, and wanted to hit him. Instead she renewed her sunscreen lotion, and turned over on her side with her back to him, opening her book again.

Later she dozed off, her bikini top undone to let the sun on to her back, her head pillowed in her arms. She woke to feel a warm finger running gently up her spine. It paused at the top, and then was joined by other fingers as it slowly stroked down again, stopping at the edge of her minute stretch pants. She ought to stop him, of course. Instead she lay still, her eyes shut, keeping her breathing even as his hand lightly caressed her hip, then explored the inward curve of her waist, and moved down again skimming over the bikini to her thigh. There it lingered briefly before returning to her back, this time with a firmer touch, his palm exploring the texture of her skin, the thumb kneading now and then, the fingers teasing at the hollows and finding the beginning of the soft swell of her breasts.

At last he paused and surprised her by doing up the clip of her top. Then his fingers rested lightly on her nape, and she knew he had shifted closer. She could feel his body heat mingled with the heat of the sun, and his leg was against hers. 'Karen,' he said, his lips touching her cheek. 'You can stop pretending to be asleep now. How about some lunch?'

She turned on to her back, opening her eyes. His hand was still behind her, holding her, and he was looking at her mouth. Her lips felt dry. She touched them with her tongue, and then flushed, realising what a provocative gesture it was. Hastily, she said, 'Yes, I could do with lunch.'

His gaze shifted to her eyes, and he gave her an ironic smile. 'Right, come on then.' He stood up and pulled her to her feet, and linked his fingers firmly in hers as they walked.

Karen slipped a muslin shirt on over her swimsuit, partly because it was marginally cooler inside, and partly because Drew's interested gaze was tending to dwell on her exposed figure, and the faint glitter in his eyes made her breathless and uncomfortable. They had egg and cheese sandwiches, and didn't bother setting the table, but Drew pulled a bottle of sparkling wine from the fridge and opened it, bringing out two stemmed glasses they had last used at Christmas. Karen laughed at him. 'What's the celebration for?' she asked as he poured the pale liquid into her glass.

'Because you and I are alone together, and not fighting,' he told her, filling his own glass. He lifted it in a toast and said, 'To us and the future, Karen ... whatever it holds.'

She couldn't quite smile. The future seemed precarious and uncertain as yet. But she raised her glass silently to his and drank.

They finished the bottle afterwards, sitting on the beach under one of the trees while the sun was at its hottest, and then went for a walk, energetically climbing to the top of the cliff. The path was steep and in some places little more than a series of crude steps cut in the sandstone, and over the last few yards Karen complained that she would never get there.

Drew took her hand, hauling her after him, and as she stepped on to the worn grass at the top, he pulled her into his arms, kissed her briefly on the lips and said, 'There. You've made it!'

Flushed and panting, she leaned on him and said, 'Shouldn't we plant a flag, or something?'

He laughed and released her, and she promptly subsided on the ground, sitting with her forearms slackly resting on her raised knees, her gaze firmly fixed on the sea. Drew came down beside her, an arm carelessly flung about her shoulders. 'You're OK, aren't you?'

'Yes.' She gave him a quick, nervous smile. 'Just out of condition, I guess. The last few years I've been too busy to exercise much.'

'Building up the business?'

'That's right.'

'Is it important to you?'

'Yes, it is. It makes me feel successful, I suppose ... as though I can do things, like a competent person. It's been good for me.'

'You've certainly changed a lot,' he commented.

'You have, too. We're really two different people, aren't we?'

'Some things are still the same.'

She kept her gaze on the view, the dark line on the horizon that separated sea and sky, the restless swells that became white-edged breakers as they neared the long sweep of the shore. 'No,' she said. 'Nothing's really the same.' She was still wildly attracted to him, and once that had been enough to make her fling herself into his arms without heed to any possible repercussions. But not now.

Drew said softly, 'Isn't it?' His hand tightened on her shoulder and he turned her face to his. She tried to stop him, her fingers closing on his wrist. He smiled and took no notice, until she dug her nails into his skin and began to struggle in earnest. She heard the sharp intake of his breath, and then they were fighting a silent, vicious little battle, and she knew she had roused his temper. The outcome was inevitable, of course. He pushed her back to the ground, her wrists imprisoned by his hands, and then his mouth was on her's, hot and hard and angry.

She was angry too, and even when the kiss gentled and became coaxing and urgent, she managed to withhold any response. She had stopped fighting him, but her mouth remained closed against him, her body rigid as stone. At last he wrenched his mouth away, and groaned, *No! Not this way!* He dropped his head on her shoulder, his face against her throat, muttering something she didn't catch. Her wrists were released, and she instinctively brought her hands to his head and shoulders, holding him. She stared up at the blue of the sky overhead, and gently fingered his hair, and for a long time they lay there unmoving.

At last he rolled away from her, lying on his back with an arm over his eyes. 'I didn't intend to do that,' he said.

'I know. It's all right.'

She sat up, and he followed suit. 'You're very generous,' he said.

Karen shook her head. He had a lot more to forgive than a stolen kiss. She was in no position to start holding grudges. She knew she had angered him, and the retaliation had really been fairly mild.

After a while, he said, 'Do you have any contact with your people?'

'My people?'

'Your aunt and uncle. I went to them after you left, asking for an address. They swore they hadn't heard from you. Was it true?'

'Yes. It was true.'

'I thought you would have gone to them.'

'No.' A faint, bitter smile touched her mouth. 'They were only too pleased to wash their hands of me when I married you. I did phone Aunt Ada, just to let her know I was all right. She wasn't even interested. The only thing that bothered her was that I might be looking for help. She said they'd done all they could for me, and if I'd made a mess of my marriage it was none of their affair. I couldn't expect any more from them.'

'They didn't tell me you'd phoned. Your uncle said they hadn't heard from you at all. He seemed relieved that you'd left me a note.' With a careful lack of expression, he added, 'At least we knew that you hadn't had an accident or been murdered.'

Karen digested that, without bitterness. 'Maybe she didn't tell him. Uncle George had a strong sense of responsibility. He died a few years ago. I saw the notice in the papers.'

'I know. I went to the funeral. You weren't there.'

She had telephoned, said she would come, but Aunt Ada had told her not to. She had her own family, she said, and Karen wasn't needed. Wasn't wanted, was the unspoken message. She had sent flowers.

'I saw the wreath you sent,' he told her. 'The florist said you'd paid cash, and there was no address.'

'Aunt Ada didn't want me there,' she said baldly.

He looked at her and said slowly, 'I had the impression you'd had a pampered childhood. But it wasn't happy, was it?'

'No, it wasn't happy. It was physically comfortable, and I was lucky in that. There wasn't even any suggestion that I should leave school until I had passed the University Entrance and Bursary exams. Uncle would have willingly supported me through university. In that way he was generous. I don't have any right to blame them, just because they couldn't love me, too.'

'I loved you,' he said with quiet violence. 'But that wasn't enough for you, was it? You were used to money and comfort, and I couldn't give it to you.'

She couldn't answer, her heart beating hard and fast, her face flushing with distress. Was that what he had thought, all these years? She supposed it must have been, and if she denied it, he would start probing again, demanding the truth.

'Did you want to go to university?' Drew asked after a while. 'You never said so.'

'I wanted to get a job as soon as possible, to be independent.'

'And instead, you married me.'

She had wanted him more than anything else. Or perhaps, she thought, looking back clear-eyed at her teenage self, she had just wanted above all to be loved. That was what had really sent her into his arms, giving everything in a headlong, immature desire to have someone take and return all the bottled-up loving that no one else had wanted.

'It wasn't exactly what I'd planned,' she admitted. 'Or you, either, was it?'

'I never regretted it, Karen,' he said. 'Unlike you.'

She looked down at her clasped hands, trying to formulate words to answer him.

'Come on,' he said, getting up abruptly. 'Shall we walk down by the road?'

CHAPTER NINE

THE ROUTE away from the cliff was across a grassy expanse, through a small stand of kanuka and kahikatea and totara, and then back to the beach by way of the dusty, metalled road. They walked in silence, keeping to the grass verge whenever possible. Karen had put on sandals after lunch, but the stones tended to make their presence felt through the thin soles, and smaller ones worked their way inside. Twice she had to stop and shake them out, and the second time she staggered and Drew steadied her with a hand on her arm.

He removed his hand immediately when she stood upright again. He reached up to hold a branch back for her that overhung the road, and as she brushed past him his hand briefly touched her waist, but that was all.

By tacit consent they headed for the beach on their return, and made for the water, shedding sandals and shirts as they went. It was blessedly cool and soothing, an antidote for tension, and they stayed in for a long time. Karen swam out beyond the breakers to float on her back, lazily staring at the sky. After a while Drew surfaced beside her and said, 'You're drifting out. Be careful.'

She looked towards the shore and saw that it was a long way off. Reluctantly she turned over and began to swim towards it. Drew kept pace, and eventually they reached the shallows and walked up the beach to where the rug and their towels still lay. Karen was panting a little, pleasantly exhausted and cool, but ready to enjoy the sun again. She didn't bother to dry herself but lay on her back, one knee slightly bent, and watched Drew with unconscious pleasure as he stood rubbing a towel over his wet hair and face, with salt droplets coursing

down his body. He threw the towel on the sand and lay
beside her on his stomach. 'You're losing a pin,' he
remarked casually, and lifted a hand to push it back into
her hair. 'And getting a little pink at the edges.' His
finger brushed her shoulder. 'Where's your sunscreen?'

'I can't be bothered,' she said. 'It's over there.'

He reached across her and picked the bottle up and
unscrewed the cap. Pouring some of the liquid into his
palm, he spread it over her shoulders and down her
upper arms. 'Here, too,' he said, touching her again, just
above the top of her bikini.

'I'll do it,' she said, trying to take the bottle from him.

He smiled, but there was a scarcely hidden ruthless
quality in it. 'Don't be such a prude.' His fingers
smoothed a line of lotion across the soft flesh, moving
with exquisite slowness. 'There.' He put back the cap
and tossed the bottle on to the sand and lay down again,
his head turned towards her.

Her skin tingled pleasantly where he had touched it,
and her pulses were hurrying. She groped for her
sunglasses and put them on, wishing he didn't disturb
her so much, and so easily, hoping that he wouldn't
know the effect he was having on her.

'What's the time?' she asked.

'I don't know. Does it mater? I left my watch in the
house.'

'When will Holly be home?'

'Probably lateish. About six, maybe seven. It'll still be
light.'

'Is she invited to the barbecue?'

'Yes. Leo asked me to pass an invitation on to Suzie
and Sandy and their kids, too.'

She should finish her book but she realised that she
had taken it back to the house at lunchtime and
forgotten it. She closed her eyes, and lapsed into silence.
The sun was still hot, although it was after three. She
supposed it would be wise to move into the shade of the
tree, but the sun was pleasant, and the water was always

there to cool off in.

Later she had another dip, and came back to find Drew sitting up and watching her. 'I've become habituated to supervising,' he explained. 'Anyway, you shouldn't really swim alone. No one should.'

'There are other people about,' she pointed out.

'They're not watching. You could easily be missed if you got into trouble.'

'I'm a pretty good swimmer.'

'Yes, I know. School champion, weren't you?'

'Fancy you remembering that.' She put a towel about her shoulders and said, 'I'm thirsty, I think I'll go back to the house for a drink. Can I bring you anything?'

'I'll come with you.'

Drew poured fruit juice and placed ice in the glasses, and they sat on the step where the house shaded them a little, and sipped thirstily.

'I think I'll have a shower,' Karen said when she had finished. 'My hair needs washing again.'

'Why did you bother doing it this morning?' Drew asked.

She had done it mainly to avoid him, she remembered. 'I couldn't bear it any longer,' she answered. 'Besides, this morning I gave it a proper treatment. This time I'll just shampoo it and use an ordinary conditioner. It really needs to be pampered every day, with all this sand and sun and salt water.'

When she had showered she pulled on a pair of bikini briefs and a short towelling wrap, and peeped into the living area to find out if Drew was about. Seeing no one, she decided he had probably returned to the beach, and she went out to the steps, holding her hair brush.

She had sat on the lower step where the sun still warmed the wood and would dry her hair, before she saw him lounging against the outside wall in the shade, another glass of juice in his hand. He wasn't wearing his shirt, but had donned a pair of jeans.

He turned and smiled at her, a smile of intimacy such as they used to exchange when they were married.

'I thought you'd gone back to the beach,' she said. She looked down at the brush in her hand, decided it was silly to change her mind now, and began smoothing it over her hair. Drew ambled over to sit on the top step behind her and after a while the brush was removed from her hand, and he took over.

Karen sat with closed eyes, enjoying the sensuous feel of it, the firm, regular rhythm. She was almost asleep when he said, softly, 'It's nearly dry. Is that enough?'

'Mm,' she said, unwilling to break the spell by talking. 'Thank you.'

He put down the brush, and spread the long hair over his denim-clad thighs, lifting the strands gently, feeling the texture. 'I'd forgotten,' he said, 'how fine and silky it is.'

She didn't move, and he went on, keeping his voice low. 'I'd forgotten the feel of your skin . . . like a pearl, firm but with a satin surface. This morning, I wanted to go on stroking your skin forever. But I hadn't forgotten what kissing you was like. It's still the same. Your mouth was always so soft I was afraid of hurting you, and so responsive that I couldn't help doing it. I remember how it used to look after we'd made love—like a bruised rose. And I always felt guilty over it, and you always laughed and said "Don't be silly, darling, I love the way you kiss me, I love everything you do to me".'

Karen began to tremble. She kept her eyes closed tightly against the flood of memory he was evoking.

'I guess I've been fantasising today,' he said, 'pretending that we'd always been together, after all, that you still wanted me. Sometimes—like this morning, when I touched you and you didn't resist—you seemed to be entering into the fantasy, too. When you reminded me that nothing is really the same, it was a bit like waking a sleep-walker. I was having a nice dream, and you shattered it. You know, for years after you left me, I used to do that. I'd dream about making love to you, and I'd put out my hand in the bed to touch you, and you weren't there.'

Her throat ached. 'Me, too,' she whispered. Night after night she had dreamt and wept and fought the insistent longing to go back, confess, ask for his forgiveness, start again. But she hadn't dared ...

For a long moment he sat still and silent. They weren't touching, except for the pale strands of her hair that trailed across his knees. His eyes were fixed on her hair, and hers looked into the distance. Almost inaudibly, he said, 'Karen—come inside with me.'

She didn't answer immediately. Time seemed suspended, the high calls of the seagulls and the distant shouts of children playing on the beach the only sounds. Even the sea seemed hushed.

He was doing nothing to persuade her, only waiting. And she knew that her answer would be accepted without argument. He was giving her a chance to begin again. It was surely more than she deserved. He had offered her Holly, and now he was offering himself. No conditions, and no strings. She had been sure that his love must have died years ago, that she must have killed it, and yet he still wanted her.

And she wanted him, loved him. It was true that they had almost become two different people, but she loved the later Drew at least as much as she had loved the younger one, perhaps more. Sometimes he was bitter and lashed out at her, but she felt he was entitled to that. With Holly he was strong and tender, humorous and kind, firm and patient. She liked everything about him. And he still had the power to make her melt with longing at a touch, a word, and set her blood racing and her skin tingling with the lightest kiss.

Everything that she wanted was hers for the taking, if she would only say the right word. Her heart thudded and her throat was dry. 'Yes,' she said, not turning her head. 'Yes, let's go in.'

He let out his breath in a long sigh, and reached down and clasped her hand in his. He got up and backed into the house, taking her with him, and as he drew her closer, reached behind her to snap shut the door. After the sunshine outside it seemed dark, and she could only see him as a dim shape. His hands slid up her arms and rested at the sides of her face, and smoothed back her hair and tipped her head until he could find her mouth, pressing a long, sweet, deliberately gentle kiss on her parted lips. Her hands went to his waist and moved over his bare back, and his kiss became more passionate on her mouth.

He broke away and fanned her hair out with his hands, watching it fall on her shoulders, then he brushed it away from her face again and tipped her head back with one hand and kissed her throat. She moaned and he came back to her mouth, and then took her hand in his and led her into the front bedroom where he slept alone in the big bed. She hesitated momentarily in the doorway and he smiled and said, 'Don't be shy, darling,' and gave her a little tug forward as he shut the door behind them.

She smiled sheepishly back at him, and said, 'It's been a long time.'

'Too long,' he agreed, bringing her into his arms again. 'Far, far too long.' He touched her lips with his, and ran his hands over the towelling that covered her. He held her waist with one arm, and pushed back the robe from her shoulder and put his lips to the warm flesh. Instinctively she pressed herself against him, but when he raised his head a little to put his lips to the hollow of her throat, she whispered, 'Drew!'

'Mm?'

His tongue was exploring the soft hollow, his arm urging her towards the bed. She pushed away a little, trying to make him listen. 'Drew . . . I'm not on the Pill.'

His head lifted, the blaze of passion in his eyes receding slightly. Then he smiled and kissed her nose.

'All right, sweetheart,' he said. 'I'll take care of it.' His mouth found hers again, and she quelled a tiny cold start of surprise and returned his kiss with an almost fierce abandon. His hand pulled at the tie that held the wrap together. It parted, and he peeled the whole thing off her shoulders and let it drop to the floor.

She gasped, flushing wildly, and he gave a low chuckle and swept her up into his arms and deposited her on the bed, coming down to join her immediately, his leg thrown across hers, his hand under her chin as he kissed her again. When he raised his head, his gaze swept down the length of her body, and he said, 'You're lovely. Even lovelier than I remembered.'

'I've lost weight,' she reminded him. 'You kept implying that I was too skinny.'

He shook his head. 'You're not too skinny. You're perfect. Perfect.' His hands skimmed her with the absorption of a connoisseur examining a work of art, even, as he turned her in his arms, lingering briefly on the almost invisible little scars that faintly marred the skin of her upper thighs and her shoulder blades. She knew he had noticed them, and stiffened, but this time he didn't comment. When he began kissing her body, she thought he pressed his lips to each one, but he was kissing her everywhere, igniting tiny fires that coalesced into one incandescent flame. She was consumed by it, wanted to consume him too, wanted to touch him, hold him, as he was holding her. She wrapped her arms about his neck and arched closer, and he groaned aloud, the sound muffled against her throat, and lifted himself away from her to pull at the fastener on his jeans. Then he froze, listening, and swore under his breath. Karen's eyes widened, as she heard it too, Holly's clear young voice, and the more distant voices of Jason and Katrina.

Bare feet thumped up the steps, and they heard the outer door open. Holly called, 'Daddy? Karen?' Karen bolted upright in the bed, grabbing the cover around her, her eyes wide with horrified surprise, and Drew leapt off the bed, threw her wrap at her and crossed the room to the door in one lightning second. He stood there with his hand on the wood, holding it shut while Karen hurriedly hauled on the robe and stumbled out of the bed, hastily trying to straighten the rumpled cover.

'Never mind that,' he whispered, and opened the door, saying, 'Hello, chicken. Have a good time?'

'Great. We found this real neat island, and ... Hi, Karen.' She flashed her mother a dazzling smile as Karen emerged from Drew's room trying to appear perfectly at ease. 'We had a picnic at the top of this hill, and you could see the sea for miles around, and it was as though we were the only people in the whole *world* ...'

Drew cocked a rueful eyebrow at Karen over Holly's oblivious head, and Karen almost giggled. Holly, at least, found nothing untoward in Karen being with Drew in his room, or else she was simply too full of her adventurous day to have even noticed.

They had to go to the barbecue, of course. Holly wouldn't have missed it for anything, scorning the suggestion that she might be tired and ready for an early night. She sat between Drew and Karen tucking away vast quantities of fish, steak, chops, sweet corn and baked potatoes, and later went running down to the beach to play in the dark with the other children present. Drew put his arm around Karen and pulled her close to lean against his shoulder as someone began to strum a guitar and sing. Later, everyone joined in. Cans of beer were passed around from a crate on the ground near the barbecue, and Carol offered wine from a flagon or soft drinks to those not having beer.

Karen settled for some wine, in a peanut-butter glass with a picture of Mickey Mouse on it, and Drew was drinking beer. The young men with their friends had congregated in a group from which hoots and shouts of laughter occasionally emanated. But one of them had politely offered a plate of salad earlier on to Karen and

Drew, and watching Carol having a quiet word with them after a bit of horseplay had sprayed beer on to nearby guests, Karen noted their sheepish expressions and realised that they were still amenable to parental disapproval.

Suzie and Sandy came and sat close by, and while Drew asked them about their day, Karen excused herself and asked Carol to direct her to the toilet.

'Through the house and just by the back door, on the porch,' Carol told her.

All the doors were open. She found her way with no trouble, and was washing her hands when she heard male voices in the kitchen.

'Where is it, then?'

'Dad said he shoved them under the table. Might as well take the lot. Carry one carton each.'

'Nah, Mum wouldn't like it. One at a time, eh?'

'Y'reckon? Yeah, s'pose so.'

Karen heard scraping and a faint, tinny rattle as the boys evidently dragged out a carton of beer. Then one of them said, 'Hey, what about that Drew fellah, eh? Does all right, doesn't he?'

'You mean his girlfriend? Yeah. Bit upmarket for you, boy.'

His brother guffawed. 'She's not bad, though. And remember that redhead last year? And whatsername—Maggie? The one with the——'

'Yeah, I remember *her*!' The answer came enthusiastically as their voices receded down the hall. 'She was *really* something, wasn't she ...?'

Karen stood holding a towel, her face in the slightly spotty mirror before her reflecting blank shock. How stupid, how gullible, she had been! Fancy at her age, not knowing better. She wasn't the only woman Drew had brought here. He made a habit of sharing his holidays with some attractive female. It had merely been convenient to ask her to be his companion this year. And perhaps he had found an added piquancy in the fact that she was his legal wife. All the time she had thought he was showing such consideration, not forcing her to commit herself to a future relationship, he had only been making sure that *he* wasn't getting in deeper than he wanted to. Frustrating for him that it had taken her so long to agree to share his bed ... and then Holly had spoiled it. No wonder she hadn't been surprised to see Karen in her father's bedroom. She was probably used to a constant procession of women coming and going. Dressed in the sexy nightgowns he bought for them, no doubt, she thought viciously, recalling the one he had purchased from her shop.

How *could* he blatantly parade his affairs in front of his daughter! And how many temporary 'aunts' had there been besides the Aunty Maggie Holly had so casually mentioned?

Furiously she stalked through the house and back to the barbecue, bitterly regretful that she couldn't start screaming like a fishwife and have it out with Drew then and there. She sat by Suzie, away from Drew, and began chatting, ignoring Drew's puzzled, quizzical glance from Suzie's other side. For the rest of the evening, until she could decently say, 'Let's go,' she kept away from him.

Of course it was impossible to have a row, with Holly about. She walked between her parents all the way back to the house, and the walls were thin. It would have to wait, Karen realised. She made to follow Holly to their room, but Drew caught her arm and said in her ear, 'Come to my room?'

She shook her head, not trusting herself to speak.

With laughter in his voice, he brushed the side of her neck with his lips and murmured, 'Later then, if you're shy.'

'No,' she said almost inaudibly, and he grasped both her arms and turned her to face him. 'What's the matter?' he asked, frowning.

'I'm tired,' she said, her voice clipped. 'Goodnight, Drew.'

Surprise must have prevented him from stopping her. She managed quite easily to evade his hold and fled into the bedroom where Holly was searching for her pyjama top. She managed to use the child as a protection until they were both in bed and the house was quiet. Much later she heard soft movements in the outer room, and then the door opened very quietly. She lay with her eyes closed, pretending to sleep. He stood there for several minutes before he silently closed the door again and went away.

He was in a black mood next day. He tried not to show it to Holly, but she said shrewdly to Karen, 'Daddy doesn't want to go. It's been a gorgeous holiday, hasn't it? The best I've ever had.'

Karen smiled and agreed but, like Drew, she couldn't wait to leave. The day had turned out bleak and unsummery, and the sea was grey and choppy. Drew made the weather an excuse to leave early, before lunch. For most of the way he drove in taciturn silence, and when Holly complained of hunger he bought take-aways so that they could eat in the car and not waste time.

When he stopped at Karen's place, he said curtly to Holly, 'Wait in the car, chicken,' and got out to take Karen's bag from the boot, slamming it shut.

Karen kissed Holly goodbye, trying to smile naturally. 'Thank you again for the presents,' she said.

'You, too,' Holly answered. The Spanish doll in its cellophane box was on the seat beside her. Touching it, Holly added, 'She's beautiful!'

'Here's something else for you.' Karen pressed a palm-sized tissue-wrapped parcel into her hand. 'I promise it doesn't pong any more.'

Holly unwrapped the sea egg, and looked at its blue-green patterned surface, now perfectly dry and clean. 'No, it's really pretty,' she agreed. 'Thank you.'

Drew had carried Karen's case to the door and was waiting impatiently for her to open it. She took the key from her handbag as she hurried towards him.

She thought he would drop the case and go, but instead he put it down just inside the door, and taking her arm, pushed her into the lounge. 'Now,' he said grimly as he released her and stood facing her, 'will you just tell me what all this is about?'

'All what?' she said frostily. She hadn't expected him to be the aggressor. It threw her off balance.

'Why I've been getting the cold shoulder since last night,' he said with exasperation. 'What the hell are you playing at, Karen? You must be the world's champion tease! If you've deliberately set out to drive me crazy, at least tell me why! Because I don't know what I'm supposed to have done!'

'I don't like being one of a crowd!' she snapped.

Drew looked totally bewildered. 'What on earth do you mean?'

'I mean that if you wanted some diversion on your holiday, you should have taken someone else. Someone like your friend Maggie, or the redhead you had in tow last year.'

'Maggie,' he said, after a moment. 'I would have told you about Maggie——'

'When?' she asked bitingly. 'After you'd got me into your bed? Would you have told me how my performance compared with hers—and with last year's girl, and all the other girls——'

He gave a crack of angry laughter. 'This is *ridiculous*! Who on earth have you been talking to? Surely Suzie didn't fill you up with all this nonsense?'

'Suzie had nothing to do with it. Your friends have been remarkably discreet. I happened to overhear a conversation, that's all. It was very enlightening.'

'Apparently,' he said sarcastically. 'It was also way off the mark.' He looked suddenly thoughtful and alert. 'My God!' he exclaimed, and a surprised grin crossed his face. 'You're jealous!'

'I am *not jealous*!' she snapped. 'I'm concerned about Holly.'

'*Holly!*' He looked confused. 'What does all this have to do with Holly?'

'Don't you have any moral scruples at all? Do you suppose it's *good* for her, having you parading your casual pick-ups through her life? What sort of an upbringing is she getting, seeing you with a different bed-mate every holiday, and heaven knows how many in between? What sort of a father are you? I don't think you're fit to look after a girl of her age.'

The humour in his eyes disappeared. 'And what gives you the right to say so?'

'I'm her mother!'

'It took you a long time to remember it!'

Karen blenched, faltering.

'You're a Sunday mother!' he said. 'A part-time parent who only has to be pleasant for a day or two a week, and treat her like a pet. Being a real parent is a lot more than having fun and buying love with expensive presents.'

'I am not buying her love!'

'Of course you are!' he argued. 'You spoil her abominably. Everything she takes a fancy to, you get for her. You're Santa Claus and the Fairy Godmother rolled into one.'

'Because *you're* too *mean* to get her what she wants. I noticed it the very first time I saw you together. You've got plenty of cash, but you talked to her as though you had to count every cent you spend.'

His voice hard, he said, 'Then maybe she'll grow up with a more realistic view of life than her mother had!'

Stunned, she couldn't retort before he went on. 'I don't want her to get the idea that money grows on trees, or that she can have everything she wants for the asking. I won't always be around to fund her, and it isn't good for anyone to imagine they don't have to work and save for what they want. She gets pocket money, and I'm trying to teach her to budget it so that she has the satisfaction of getting things with her own efforts. That's what being a *responsible* parent is all about, Karen. I have the job of teaching her to be a useful, happy person. I can't be Mr Nice Guy all the time. *I* can't afford to let her twist me round her little finger, and I certainly can't give her the moon and anything else she asks for. You get that role,' he ended bitterly.

Her eyes flashed. 'If you resent it so much, why did you offer it to me?' she asked him.

'I told you why.'

'Because Holly needed a mother figure? There doesn't seem to have been a shortage of candidates.'

'They weren't you! Believe it or not, I had this idiotic notion that maybe some day we could be a family again. That's why I asked you to come with us to the beach.'

'You mean . . . come back to you?'

He looked at her broodingly. 'Surely it's occurred to you. We weren't doing too badly together until . . .'

'Until last night.'

His face hardened again. 'And last night someone mentioned Maggie—and you got some twisted ideas about me.'

'Holly told me that "Aunty Maggie" lived with you. I thought at the time that she was a middle-aged housekeeper.'

Drew tried to hide his amusement. 'Maggie was hardly that,' he admitted. 'She was extraordinarily beautiful, quite like a film star, as Holly once pointed out. But under the glamour and the stunning clothes and make-up she was a real homebody, with a well-developed domesticated streak. She liked nothing better than to spend the afternoon in the kitchen with Holly, making gooey sweets and cream cakes.'

Already consumed with the jealousy she had denied, Karen asked tartly, 'Are you telling me she didn't share your bed?'

Drew said, watching her, 'No, I'm not telling you that.'

'I'll bet she was a tigress,' Karen said with waspish sarcasm. 'She seems to have been good at everything.'

He gave her a hard look from under his brows, and she flushed. 'Holly said she got married,' she told him. 'How could you have let such a paragon slip through your fingers? What did your rival have that you didn't?'

'He was never my rival. She didn't meet him until after we parted.' Curtly, he said, 'Look, sit down for a minute.'

'Holly's waiting for you,' she protested as he took her hand and led her unwillingly to the sofa.

'She'll be all right for a while. This won't take long.' He made her sit down, and settled himself half facing her. 'For God's sake, listen, Karen, and try to understand.'

She looked down at her fingers, linking them in her lap.

'I met Maggie three years ago,' he said, 'at some party. You couldn't miss Maggie, and like most men I was quite taken by her looks. We got talking and we liked each other. I'd been seeing her for quite a while before I introduced her to Holly. They got on like a house on fire from the start, and after a while it seemed ... natural that Maggie should move in with us. She was a nice girl and I was fond of her, and I'd been alone for a long time. It was really very pleasant to have someone besides Holly to come home to, and Maggie was happy to take over the domestic side of things. It lasted that way for eighteen months, and then she got ... restless. She knew how things were with ... us, but she wanted to have a baby of her own. And quite naturally she didn't want it born outside wedlock.'

'Why didn't she ask you to divorce me?'

'She did.' He paused. 'I've often asked myself why I wouldn't do it. She accused me of using her as a convenient housekeeper and mistress. And in a way, I guess she was right. I could only say that I hadn't planned it that way, and in the beginning she'd been quite happy to go along with the arrangement. But of course it's true that I treated her very unfairly. I've felt guilty about it ever since.'

With reason, Karen thought, feeling a reluctant stirring of sympathy for Maggie. Tartly she said, 'Your marriage must have been a useful buffer when you didn't want to get too involved.'

'I didn't see it like that,' he denied harshly. 'I just ... as long as I didn't know what had happened to you, I couldn't bring myself to get a divorce. I guess I still felt married to you. It was impossible to imagine being married to anyone else.'

'Holly must have missed her,' Karen suggested. 'After eighteen months.'

'Yes, she did of course. Holly's relationship with her was so good that it almost made me do it. I think half of my attraction for Maggie was the fact that I had a child. She doted on kids ... well, that's what broke us up. She ... Maggie was very good about it, very generous. She spent a lot of time with Holly after the break-up, taking her out, having her at her place.'

A surrogate Sunday mother, Karen thought.

'But then,' he continued, 'she met someone and wanted to get married. And as she explained to me, he wouldn't have minded if the child had been her own, but he drew the line at her seeing the child of her ex-lover. I couldn't blame him. And Holly bounced back quite quickly after the initial upset. The break had been a gradual one, thanks to Maggie. I'll always be grateful to her for that ... and all the rest.'

She wished he hadn't said so. She, too, ought to be grateful, she supposed, to the unknown woman who had given Holly a happy and almost normal family life for eighteen months. But all she could feel was raging envy.

'And who,' she enquired coolly, 'was the raving redhead you had at the beach last year?'

'Redhead?' he said, frowning.

'Surely you remember?' she said, her voice rising. 'She seems to have made quite an impression on the rest of the male population.'

He snapped his fingers. 'Oh, yes, at the barbecue! Carol and Leo threw a beach party last year, too. There was a girl there ...'

'I had the impression she was *your* girl.'

He looked at her exasperatedly. 'We met that evening. We spent some time together the next day, that's all. There was nothing to it, but she was fun and we enjoyed ourselves. I don't even remember her name. Look, Karen. There were girls from time to time. It's been ten years, for heaven's sake! Did you think that there wouldn't have been anyone? The only one Holly ever knew was Maggie. I don't suppose you've been totally without male companionship, either. Is there any point in our swapping the details of our social lives?'

She shook her head, not looking at him. 'I suppose not. It was only for Holly's sake ...'

'Am I supposed to believe that?' he asked.

But she wasn't ready to meet the implications of that remark. She stood up. 'She's waiting for you. Hadn't you better go?'

'You're right, I can't keep Holly waiting too long. But don't think we're finished, Karen. There's still a lot we have to say to each other. Think about it.'

CHAPTER TEN

KAREN had to go back to work the following day. Gretta had acquired a new boyfriend—whose couth and varied charms she described in breathless detail over the course of the morning—and a pair of startling fuchsia-coloured ankle-length bloomers. A scarf in the same shade was bound with gold rope about her head and she wore matching lipstick and nail varnish. She looked like an escapee from a harem. Karen, who enjoyed Gretta's adventurous taste in clothes and seldom failed to remark on a new addition to her assistant's wardrobe, didn't even notice until lunchtime.

'Thought you mustn't have liked it,' Gretta said with relief, when Karen confessed to her unusual lapse of observation and belatedly commented on the fuchsia pants. 'What's the matter with you, anyway? Holiday hangover? You've been away with the fairies all day.'

'Too much sun, I guess,' Karen said lightly.

'Yeah, you've got a tan all right. Funny, you lying about in the sun trying to get brown, and me trying to keep out of it so I won't go any darker.'

Karen smiled. 'Silly, isn't it? Nobody's satisfied with the way they are, I suppose.'

'Where did you go?'

Karen told her, and hastily changed the subject. The next obvious question was 'who with?' and she didn't want to answer that.

She was ashamed of the way she had flown at Drew without giving him a chance to defend himself. And deep down she knew full well that her motives had not had a great deal to do with any danger to Holly's moral development. She had been furious because she thought he was putting her—his wife, after all—on the same level

160

as a host of unimportant women with whom he had had temporary liaisons. And it hadn't been like that at all.

He had hinted that he wanted her back. And perhaps not entirely for Holly's sake. Not that she should be hurt if Holly was the main reason. Karen had made him responsible for Holly, and he had every right—even a duty—to put her first.

She ought to be grateful that he wanted her at all, for any reason and on whatever terms. It wasn't everyone who got a second chance like this. The only thing to do was grab it with both hands.

She saw him when he brought Holly round for her weekly visit, but he didn't seem to be inclined to make an opportunity for private discussion. She wondered sometimes if he had changed his mind, regretted bringing up the subject after all. She knew he didn't wholly trust her, and knew that he had reason . . .

It was February before he phoned the shop and asked if she was free that evening, and could he take her out to dinner. She said yes, and spent the rest of the day in a fever of anticipation. When he called for her before she locked up, Gretta was just leaving. Today she wore a vivid orange skirt with an assortment of blouses and sleeveless garments over it in a mixture of pink and green hues. She had skewered her piled-up glossy hair with Japanese-style combs and tassels in equally brilliant colours, and Drew gave her a faintly startled smile as she passed him. Watching her spectacular progress, he murmured to Karen, 'Does she often come in dressed like that?'

Karen laughed. 'Variations of it, yes. It adds a bit of colour to the place. I only wish I had the looks to carry some of the combinations she can get away with. Mint green and purple for instance. On most people it would look indescribably awful. On her it looks fantastic.'

'I'll take your word for it. And there's nothing wrong with your looks.'

She smiled rather uncertainly at him, and went to get

her bag. She had seen at a glance that he was wearing the shirt she had made for him. Coming out of the back room, she asked him, 'Would you mind taking me home first? I'd like to change. Where are we going?'

'It's open to discussion, but I know you used to like Chinese food. There's a Cantonese restaurant opened recently in town. Would you care to try it?'

'Sounds lovely.'

She exerted herself to be pleasant that evening. She had dressed quickly so as not to keep him waiting, but taken care with her appearance all the same, and she knew she looked attractive in beige lawn and biscuit-coloured shoes and belt. She had put on the amber and gold jewellery that Drew had given her at Christmas, and as they finished the meal with aromatic green-leaf tea, he touched one of the ear-rings with a finger and said, 'I'm glad you wore these. I've wanted to see them on you again.'

'I'm glad you wore the shirt,' she answered. 'It looks good.'

'*I* thought so.' He smiled at her. 'We haven't exchanged a cross word all evening. Isn't that some sort of record?'

'It isn't over yet. But ... I wanted to apologise for ... jumping to conclusions.'

'Let's bury the past, shall we?'

If only they could. 'A new beginning?'

For a moment he was silent. 'Would you like that?'

'Yes.' She put down the Chinese porcelain cup with its painted dragon, and swallowed nervously.

'Finished?' Drew enquired. 'Can we go back to your place?'

She nodded, and he paid their bill and held her arm lightly as they left the restaurant. He helped her into the car as if she were fragile, and she rather felt like it. Her stomach was fluttering and her bones seemed brittle and thin inside her skin.

As he followed her into her lounge, she said, 'Would you like coffee?'

'No, thanks.'

She put her small bag down carefully on a side table, and turned to face him. There was a faint, questioning smile on his face. She stood feeling rather awkward, her fingers loosely linked in front of her.

He came close to her and took her hands into his, and bent to kiss her mouth.

It started off as a light touch, hardly more than a friendly peck, but her lips moved involuntarily under his, clinging, and he slid his hands up her arms to her shoulders and then behind her to fold her closely into his arms.

She sighed into his mouth, and he brought up his hands to cradle her head in them, and lifted his mouth from hers to touch his lips briefly to her eyes and cheeks and the shallow groove below her ear. His hands eased the fabric of the lovely frock from her shoulders, and his lips lightly touched her warm flesh. She put her hands on his chest, felt the thumping of his heart, under the monogram she had embroidered on his shirt, and splayed her fingers against it. He brought his mouth back to hers, and his hands to her bared shoulders, stroking her skin, shifting her bra strap gently out of the way. Her hand shifted until her fingers encountered the tiny pearl buttons that fastened the shirt, and he murmured against her mouth, 'Undo them.' Then Karen moved in his arms, and he drew back and looked down at her troubled face. 'Too soon?' he asked her.

She nodded. 'I . . . think so. Nothing's really resolved, is it?'

'I thought we agreed on a new beginning.'

'Does that mean you won't . . . you won't ask any more questions?'

His hands fell away, and his face changed. 'I hope,' he said, 'that some day you'll tell me why you left. Because it wasn't just that I couldn't keep you in the manner to which you'd been accustomed, was it?'

She wanted to say that was it, but his hard gaze told her he wouldn't believe her.

'I hoped,' he said, 'that we'd come to trust each other as we used to.'

'I trust you,' she whispered.

'Then why don't you *tell* me?' he burst out.

Her gaze wavered and her mouth trembled. He looked angry and frustrated, and though she tried to muster courage, to begin the explanation that she knew he was entitled to, her tongue seemed glued to the roof of her mouth, and she couldn't speak.

He suddenly seized her arms, his eyes blazing into hers. 'One day,' he said, 'I'll *shake* it out of you!'

Fear blocked her throat, and translated itself into anger. 'Let me go!' She fought him, bringing up her fists and shoving at his chest.

He grabbed her wrists, holding them in one hand, and with the other he took hold of her hair and pulled back her head so that she gasped, her eyes wide and apprehensive.

'What are you frightened of?' he demanded. 'I've never hurt you in your life—in spite of the temptation.'

'You're hurting me now.'

'No.' His voice was flat, his eyes narrowed and brilliant with his anger, and something else. 'No, I'm not. Perhaps I should.'

She shivered in his hold, and he must have felt it. He gave a short, harsh laugh and released her. He was looking at her strangely. 'Oh, what the hell!' he said under his breath. 'I don't know why I bother.'

He turned, and had his hand on the doorknob before she said, 'Will I see Holly on Sunday?'

'If you want to see her,' he said, 'you can come to our place. You know the address.'

It was a small, newish house overlooking the Waitemata, only ten minutes from the city centre, but surrounded by slim silver birches, planted for quick growth while slower-growing trees and shrubs became established in their shade, and ivy ground covers. Holly had an attic-roofed room with a dormer window that she loved, and in the main bedroom a long window looked straight out over the water. Holly showed it to her, giving her a tour of the house. Karen hadn't wanted to come here, but Drew had made it a challenge. If she wanted to see Holly, she had to come. He was there, of course, but to her relief he behaved with impeccable casualness. No doubt she owed that to Holly's presence, but she was grateful for it, and although every time she accidentally looked directly at him, his glance made her heart pound uncomfortably, she had quite a pleasant day.

In response to a confidential request, she left Gretta in charge of the shop the following Saturday morning and took Holly to be fitted for her first bra. As they passed a jeweller's shop afterwards, Karen caught sight of a pair of ear-rings she fancied, and on impulse went in and tried them on. They were pearl teardrops swinging on short gold chains, and as she slipped them into her ears, Holly said, 'They suit you. I love them.'

Karen did, too. She removed them and paid for them, replacing the topaz ear-rings that Drew had given her and which today she was wearing with a soft green cotton shirtwaist dress. As she picked up the small parcel, Holly, who had been gazing into the showcases, said, 'Oh, look, aren't they nice?'

It was a pair of tiny, gold crescent moons, each with a very fine chain dangling an even smaller star. 'Could I wear those, do you think? Aren't they *neat*!'

'They're for pierced ears,' Karen pointed out.

'Oh, darn.' Her face fell, then she turned and said eagerly, 'I could have mine done, couldn't I? Lots of my friends have pierced ears. Catriona had hers done when she was only six! It's supposed to be better when you're young.'

Karen looked doubtful.

'Oh, *please*, Mummy.' Holly grabbed her arm in her agitation.

The assistant behind the counter smiled and said, 'We do it here. It's almost painless, and very hygienic and everything.'

'*Please?*'

Karen said, 'You wouldn't be able to wear ear-rings right away, you know. You have to use sleepers at first. And it would hurt a bit later.'

'Not much. I asked my friends. I've been thinking about it for ages!'

Karen was startled. 'I didn't know that.'

'Well, I never saw any ear-rings I liked so much. At least I did once, but Daddy said they were too old for me, anyway. It wouldn't take long, would it?' she turned to the shop assistant.

'Not long at all,' the woman said. 'A few minutes. And Mr Fawcett has done hundreds of them.'

In the end Karen yielded, and bought a pair of gold sleepers and the moon-and-star ear-rings. She was quite unprepared for the storm that broke over her head when she took Holly home and the child proudly showed Drew her newly pierced ears. He went white, and said ominously, 'Whose idea was this?'

'Mine,' Holly said uncertainly. 'Mummy said I could,' she added defensively. 'It's all right, Daddy, it doesn't hurt.'

Drew cast Karen a distinctly threatening look, but managed to control his temper. 'Why don't you go and put your parcels in your room,' he suggested to Holly. 'And you have some homework to do, don't you?'

'Are you angry?'

'I'm just . . . surprised,' he said. 'Run along.'

'OK.' She was subdued, but apparently relieved to escape. As soon as she had left the room, Drew turned on Karen and demanded in a furious undertone, 'Just what the *hell* do you think you're doing?'

Karen blinked. 'I don't know what you mean.'

'You know what I mean!' he contradicted. 'How dare you allow her to be mutilated——'

'*Mutilated?*' Karen choked disbelievingly. 'Don't be silly, Drew. You're over-reacting. It isn't unusual for young girls to have pierced ears. Holly said lots of her friends have . . .'

'*Holly* said! Don't you know yet that's the universal cry of every child ever born? "But all my friends have got it", or are doing it or whatever! How could you fall for that?'

'I didn't fall for anything!'

'You're still playing at being fairy godmother!' he accused her. 'Holly likes it, so Holly gets it, no matter whether it's good for her or not.'

'I wouldn't buy her anything that was bad for her!'

'Supposing she gets an infection from this amateur operation?'

'It's highly unlikely. The shop is a reputable one, and they've given us detailed instructions on how to care for her ears until they heal.'

'Oh, great!' he said sarcastically. 'And you try and tell me it's not a mutilation?'

'Technically, perhaps it is!' Karen admitted with exasperation. 'But for heaven's sake, two tiny little holes! And it happens to be true that the nicest ear-rings need pierced ears to wear them——'

'She's too *young* to wear them!'

'No, she isn't. There are suitable——'

'I am not having my daughter wearing ear-rings, Karen!'

Karen flared. 'She's my daughter, too! *I* wear them. *You* even bought me some!'

'That's different. You're a grown woman. Holly's only a little *girl.*'

Karen suddenly laughed. 'Drew, you're reacting in the classic fatherly fashion, refusing to admit that your precious little girl is growing up. I've just bought Holly her first bra. She is *not* a child any longer.'

'A *bra*?' he said, disconcerted. 'That's ridiculous! She can't need ...'

'Yes, she does. She's growing.'

'I know she's growing! But at this stage—and anyway, you had no right ...'

'Yes, I did,' Karen said firmly, lifting her chin. 'You've given me the right, Drew. You gave me the right to be her mother again, and you can't just take it back ...'

'Yes, I damn well can!' he said cuttingly. 'There isn't a judge in the country that would give legal rights to a deserting mother. You have no sense of responsibility, you never did have! I should have known better than to trust you with her again!'

The shock was so sickening, she couldn't answer him. She turned and walked straight out of the house, and blindly down the street to the main road, where she was lucky enough to just make it to a bus which was about to pull out from the stop. When she got home she was still trembling, and tears ran down her cheeks as she made herself prepare a cup of tea and drink it. Afterwards she sat for a long time staring into the empty cup, and trying not to think.

When the doorbell rang, she contemplated not answering, but it rang again, a long, insistent peal, and she wiped the back of her hand over her wet cheeks, and dragged herself down the hall.

Drew took one look at her face, and said, 'It's all right, Karen. I didn't mean it. It was just temper.'

She began to cry again, with relief, and he pulled her into his arms and she sobbed against his chest.

Later, when the tears had dried and he had steered her into the sitting-room and made her sit on the sofa, she said, 'If I'd had any idea you would object so strongly I would have waited, but ... it was the first time she'd asked my permission for anything directly, without consulting you. Maybe it went to my head.'

He frowned, looking at her in silence. Then he said

reluctantly, 'I guess maybe that's part of the problem. I'm so used to being the one to give the permission for everything, it was a bit of a shock to have Holly do something like this without my approval. And I must admit I still don't like it. I do think she's too young. But,' he shrugged, 'what's done is done.' Changing the subject, he said, 'Does she really need a bra?'

'Do you object to that, too?' she asked ironically.

Drew shook his head. 'No, of course not. I knew she was growing . . . I've talked to her, but I didn't think she needed it yet.'

'Well, yes, she does,' Karen told him. 'She'll be tender, and it will give her a little protection. And save embarrassment at school. She asked me to help her. You don't mind that, do you?'

'No.' He smiled faintly, a little rueful. 'Maybe I do, a bit,' he admitted. 'But it's natural. I'm . . . glad she's got you to ask.'

'I'm not irresponsible, Drew.'

He nodded, and put out his hand to stroke away a strand of her hair that had fallen against her cheek. His hand lingered, and curled about her nape and he leaned over and gently kissed her.

'Where is Holly?' she asked as he lifted his mouth.

'Going to a friend's place. She's invited for tea.' He brought his mouth down again on hers, and kissed her more deeply. His hands touched her lightly all over as though he wanted to make sure she was real. Then he stopped kissing her, and stayed for a long time with his arms wrapped about her tightly, his cheek against hers. Her arms were about his neck, her fingers spread on his back. Their bodies were close and warm, and they breathed in the same rhythm.

'Karen,' he said softly, 'I want you so much. Can we go upstairs?'

She nodded, and they walked up slowly, their arms about each other.

At the bedroom door she hesitated, suddenly shy of

him. He urged her gently into the room, and she caught
a glimpse of their reflection in the mirror, his arm about
her waist, her face flushed and her eyes luminous. He
turned her to him, and lifted his hands to take the pins
from her hair, placing each one carefully on the
dressing-table behind her, until the fine, soft mass was
falling about her face and shoulders. She was shaking,
and he smiled at her and began to slide her dress away
from her, finding the zip at the back and opening it
while he eased the fabric down her arms. His hands
caressed her skin, and he pulled her a little closer as the
dress slithered to the floor. 'How about undoing my
buttons for me?' he teased softly.

This time she obeyed without question. His hands
linked about her waist while he watched her slow
progress down to his waist, and took her hands in his and
pressed them to his skin. Then he tipped back her head
again with his hands and brought her mouth, open and
passionate, to his.

He swung her up in his arms and laid her on the bed,
and this time there were no interruptions and no doubts.
They made love to each other as they had in another life
long ago, when they were two other people. Everything
was just as she had remembered, only better. It was all
both strange and familiar, like one of her recurring
restless dreams. She knew what he wanted of her, and
gave it to him with frank generosity. He knew how to
evoke her most ardent responses, and used the knowledge with an almost ruthless desire to please her. It was
hours before they were sated, lying in each other's arms
on a tumbled bed, drowsily content.

'I've still got my ear-rings on, and my ring,' she said,
noticing that she had forgotten to remove the jewellery.
It was growing dark, and at some point Drew had
switched on the dim bedside lamp, and the stones shone
faintly in its glow.

'I told you I like seeing them on you,' Drew
murmured. 'They suit you . . . particularly when you're

wearing nothing else!'

She stifled a shocked laugh, and buried her face in his warm neck.

'There's one thing wrong, though,' he said, and he took her left hand and caressed the third finger.

'I still have it,' she said huskily. There wasn't even a mark where her wedding-ring had been, but it lay in her top drawer, in the tiny box embroidered sachet she had made for it.

'Where?'

She held her breath as he found it and pushed it back on to her finger.

'I want you back,' he said soberly. 'We still have things to work out, but we belong together, you and I, and our child. And I know you won't do anything to hurt Holly.'

He was still holding her hand, his finger and thumb caressing the gold band he had replaced on her finger. 'You never did have an engagement ring, did you?'

There hadn't been time for the farce of an engagement. Frightened out of her wits by her pregnancy, she had left it as late as possible to tell her aunt and uncle, and they had reacted predictably. A hurried, quiet marriage was the only solution. Karen had not really resisted. She wanted nothing more than to be with Drew for the rest of her life, and she hadn't had the courage to face having the baby alone. She had felt guilty, though, about the shelving of Drew's plans to complete his degree and try for an overseas scholarship. When he suggested he might continue his university work part-time, she had agreed eagerly and, even after Holly was born, made superhuman efforts not to interrupt him when he was studying. He had spent his savings on setting up their home with furniture and appliances, the job he had got didn't pay very much, and their rent was high, making budgeting difficult. They could have lived with Drew's mother, but to Karen's relief Drew had vetoed the idea, saying they ought to be independent from the start. She knew that Mrs Bridger was sure it was Karen's choice. She had thought when she left that probably he would move in with his mother after all, thus solving some economic, as well as other, problems.

'What are you thinking?' Drew said, tracing a line down her inner arm with his finger.

'Nothing.' Firmly she pushed aside the uncomfortable memories. 'You'll have to go and fetch Holly, won't you?'

He looked at his watch. 'I guess so. They won't mind, but I can't leave it too late. Karen—will you come home?'

'Home?'

'Yes. Where you belong. Move in with us.'

CHAPTER ELEVEN

KAREN found the nightie and panties she had sold to Drew, untouched and still in their gift box, at the bottom of a drawer, and asked suspiciously, 'Who *did* you buy them for?'

'I told Gretta,' he said blandly. 'My wife.'

'You didn't have a wife then—not that you could—could call a wife.'

With a narrow, challenging grin he admitted, 'As a matter of fact, I succumbed to a desire to score off you. I was hoping you'd be madly jealous and chagrined as hell. There wasn't anyone—but they'd look good on you.'

She didn't tell him that the effect had been all he could have hoped for. But she wore the nightdress, and watched his eyes kindle when he saw her in it. She had always known it would suit her.

Holly took her mother's moving in quite matter-of-factly, expressing satisfaction but no particular surprise. She called Karen 'Mum' or 'Mummy' about half the time now, and Karen was amused to note that she was always 'Mum' in front of Holly's friends. She seemed to have got over any resentment she might have harboured about her mother's defection, and gave every indication of being a happy, secure and almost alarmingly normal little girl.

Karen said to Drew one day, as she entered the living-room and found him staring out of the window, 'Holly wants to go to a rock concert with her friends. Are we going to let her?'

He turned. 'We'll think about it, I suppose.' He smiled and held out his hand. She put hers into it and they stood side by side, looking out of the window. 'She's growing up rapidly, isn't she?' he said.

'Yes. It'll be boyfriends next. You'll have to vet them and ask what their intentions are.'

He laughed. 'I don't think that's done any more.' He pulled her in front of him, standing behind her with his arms about her, holding her hands in front of her waist. 'Holly told me the other day that it would be nice to have a brother or sister.' His lips touched her hair. 'Has it occurred to you,' he said, 'that you're not too old to become a mother again?'

A shiver slid over her body. 'Yes, it has,' she said crisply. 'Which is why I'm taking precautions.'

There was a short, sharp silence. 'I hadn't realised that you were.'

She didn't reply to that, and after a moment he said, 'Personally, I wouldn't mind making Holly into a big sister. I think it might be good for her, and she'd love it.'

'You're the one who keeps telling me Holly shouldn't get everything she asks for!' Karen reminded him. She tugged his hands away from her waist and said, 'I have things to do.'

As she walked over to the doorway Drew said, 'Suppose *I'm* doing the asking, Karen?'

'No!' she said wildly, and fled to their bedroom.

He couldn't be serious, she thought. Drew hadn't mentioned any hankering for more children when he asked her to come back. Holly had put the idea into his head. They'd both soon forget about it.

She pulled open a drawer and tidied it unnecessarily, just for something to do. The ear-rings she had bought the day Holly had her ears pierced were still in their wrapped box. She had never worn them. She tore off the paper and regarded them, nestling against the white satin lining. They were quite beautiful.

She wore the ear-rings in bed that night, along with a

pearl satin gown that had a tiny fitted bodice, and seed pearls sewn to the narrow shoulder straps. The nightgown was soon dispensed with, but after they had made love, and she was lying across Drew's naked chest with his hand idly stroking up and down her spine, he flicked at one of the ear-rings and said, 'They're new, aren't they?'

'I bought them the day we had that row over Holly.'

He touched them again. 'Very sexy. Do you remember me telling you that your skin reminded me of pearls?' He paused a moment and then said, 'Holly showed me hers. You bought her the moon and the stars. I always knew you would, if you could.'

'So would you,' she accused him, laughing.

'But you don't want to give her a younger brother or sister?'

'No.' Karen suddenly sobered. 'That isn't the reason you invited me back, is it?' she asked.

'You know the reason,' he said. 'It had nothing to do with Holly—or very little.'

'Oh?' she said, casting him a provocative glance. 'What was it, then?'

'You know what it was!' He rolled over and held her wrists while he exacted a sweet punishment. 'God, I've done it again!' he said, looking down at the swollen redness of her mouth.

'And again . . . please!' she whispered, her eyes full of passionate invitation.

'Oh, God, yes!' he groaned, and brought his mouth back to hers, and gathered her softness into his arms.

Later she lay on her back while Drew, prone beside her, held her hand, his eyes on her face. 'Karen' he said, 'is it the boutique?'

'Is what the boutique?' she asked sleepily.

'Is that why you don't want another baby?'

She went cold, then grabbed at the excuse with both hands. 'Yes,' she said. 'I can't give it up just like that, you know. I told you how much it means to me, and it isn't as though I just ordered in stock. The whole character of the place depends on my input in design, in sewing, as well as management. I wouldn't have time for that with a young family. Even if I could afford more assistance, I wouldn't want to, because ...'

He leaned over and silenced her with a firm kiss. 'Karen,' he said, 'you're babbling. You always babbled when you were lying. Why are you lying to me?'

'It's the truth,' she said defensively.

'Some of the truth, maybe. It's understandable that you might not want another baby. But I would help— I'm fairly experienced now, remember—and Holly would be delighted to do her share. And if necessary we can afford paid help. I know you probably wouldn't want to give up your work, but if you were keen on the idea, we could work it out.'

'I've told you, I'm not!' Karen snapped.

'OK,' he said. 'It doesn't matter.'

She was relieved to hear it, but thought she detected a note of disappointment in his voice, and unwillingly she couldn't help probing further. 'Have you suddenly developed a longing for a son and heir?' she asked, her voice brittle.

'No. I just thought ... I guess I was remembering how close we were when Holly was a baby. At least ... I thought we were. And I've never forgotten what it was like being with you when she was born. I felt so wretchedly guilty seeing you in labour with our child, and I admired you so much for your courage ... *you* kept reassuring *me* that it wasn't so bad ... but then, when we were allowed to hold her ... it was the most tremendous experience of my life.'

'Mine, too,' she admitted softly.

'Yes. I swore I would never make you go through that again, and you said it was worth it. Worth everything. You talked of "next time".'

Karen lay silent, remembering that moment of profound joy, the total euphoria, and the closeness that Drew had spoken of. It had been wonderful. There was no other word for it. 'Was it worth it for you?' she said at last. 'Giving up university, your career plans, to be saddled with a wife and baby instead?'

'Yes. Yes, it was. I was satisfied. But you ... what was it you *wanted*, Karen? Why wasn't it enough for you?' He suddenly thumped his fist into the pillow. 'I've searched and searched for reasons. And you won't *tell* me! I know that you were tired, but so was I. I was too busy to spend a lot of time with the baby, I suppose I could have been more help, but then my mother was there so often ... it wasn't as though you were on your own. And you managed all right ... I thought.'

'You thought!' she echoed bitterly. 'Actually, I never made much of a housewife.'

'That didn't matter. It was a shabby old place, but you kept it clean and tidy, and I know you weren't the world's best cook when we started, but you were learning fast ... You made a home of it.'

At the cost of total exhaustion, Karen thought. Trying to keep up to her mother-in-law's standards of housekeeping, cooking and babycare, she had worn herself into the ground, though determined to hide what she thought of as her inadequacy from Drew, who was preoccupied with important examinations in the offing. There were times when she was dangerously close to screaming point. Once she had asked her doctor for help, but the tranquillisers he gave her made her slower than ever at attending to the never-ending housework, and added to her depression. If Drew noticed that she was drooping, she would smile brightly and say, 'Oh, just a bit tired. Holly woke last night.' Tired himself, he seldom stirred when the baby cried, but Karen, with a mother's instinct, never quite stopped being alert for the thin, high wail of distress, even when she was asleep.

Holly was a restless baby. She had taken months to establish a reasonable sleep pattern, and the least ailment would set her off waking in the middle of the night again. Sometimes Karen would get up several times to soothe her, and stumble back to bed only to lie listening for the next cry.

'I would rather have had you,' she said, 'than your mother.'

'I'm sorry.' He sounded baffled. 'But I wouldn't have been nearly as much use. And you know how things were.'

'I know. Oh, it wasn't your fault. Or your mother's. She did her best.'

'You were such a good mother,' Drew said. 'In spite of being so young. Too young, I know, to be tied down with a husband and family. But you were crazy about Holly, and she was beautifully looked after. I've never understood why you didn't take her with you when you left me.'

Take her! Karen thought hysterically. That was the last thing she could have done! She said painfully, 'It wasn't you I was leaving, Drew.'

She thought of that day. She'd left a note for Drew, phoned his bewildered mother and asked her in a tight, controlled voice to come right away and care for Holly, and then thrown some clothes into an overnight bag and walked out, only waiting furtively round a nearby corner until she saw Drew's mother hurry up to the house. She had never experienced such total misery before or since. As she picked up her bag and boarded a bus, she had told herself she might as well not have bothered packing anything, because her life was over, anyway. It had crossed her mind to find a convenient high bridge, but she didn't even have the energy for that. Instead she went to the bank and took out some money, part of the generous amount her uncle had given them as a wedding present to start an account towards a home of their own. She felt like a thief but knew that Drew wouldn't grudge it to her. Eventually she had found a strange town and a strange hotel and slept for twelve hours—the first good sleep she could recall since Holly's birth. And for a long time, the last. Her body had allowed her that much, but her mind, with its burden of guilt and pain and wrenching doubts, had kept her a victim to insomnia and despairing, tortured dreams in all the ensuing years, until now.

She hadn't wanted to remember the nightmare of that day. She turned away from Drew in the bed, tears welling from her eyes. He touched her shoulder and said, 'Karen?'

'Don't!' She hunched away from him, but a sob tore at her throat, and he gathered her into his arms, stilling her instinctive, convulsive struggle.

'Please,' he said, softly. 'Can't you tell me about it?'

She shook her head vehemently. 'You'd hate me.'

Perplexed, he said, 'Nothing's going to make me hate you. I was angry and bitter at you for leaving me, but even that didn't make me hate you. I love you, Karen. I can't stop loving you, even if I try . . . and I have tried. It just didn't work.'

Fear and the desire for confession—for forgiveness— fought a brief, fierce emotional battle. But suddenly she was tired of keeping her hurt and pain and guilt a secret, tired of fighting the urge to tell Drew what he wanted to know. Always their tentative rebuilding of a relationship was marred by his baffled inability to fathom what had gone wrong with their marriage the first time, and it wasn't fair to him.

'Supposing ...' she said, almost inaudibly, 'I hurt Holly?'

As soon as she said it, she felt sick with terror. Drew hadn't moved, but she could feel the shock in his rigid stillness, as he comprehended what she'd said. Then, his voice shaken, he said, 'Is *that* what it was about? You *hurt Holly*?' She heard the horror in the words, before he added, 'You couldn't have! There was nothing wrong with her.'

'I wanted to.' Her stomach crawled with shame. 'I wanted to, it was ... horrible. I was so close to doing it ... I'd had all I could take, and it was just ... I couldn't stand it any more. She'd been crying all day, off and on, and I had a headache, and the washing machine broke down. It was raining and I couldn't even get the nappies clean, let alone dry. And I couldn't find anything wrong with her, only *I couldn't stop her crying.*'

She stopped, biting her lip fiercely against the memories of that terrible, nightmarish day.

'Tell me,' Drew said quietly. His hand moved on her shoulder, stroking, and it gave her the courage to whisper her confession.

'There was nothing I could do. I tried feeding her, playing with her, putting her to bed, picking her up, rocking, walking—everything. She didn't even seem to want me at all. When I cuddled her she just threw herself away from me ... it was as if she was rejecting me.'

'Did you think of phoning the doctor?'

'She wasn't feverish or vomiting or anything. I'd had her to the doctor before when she was like that, and he examined her all over and said there wasn't anything wrong but a bit of colic, and to give her a spoonful of gripe water. He said she'd get over it by three months. But your mother just snorted and said she'd be over it when she was ready.'

'Yes, I vaguely remember that. I know she used to cry a lot. I thought all babies did.'

'Not like that. Anyway, I'd tried the stuff he gave me, and that didn't help, either. She just went on crying. She'd stop and I'd think she'd gone to sleep, and then it would start all over again. And . . . about three o'clock in the afternoon, I'd picked her up again, trying to quieten her, she kept yelling and squirming and trying to get away from me, and all of a sudden, it was just too much! Something snapped. I took her into the bedroom, and . . . and threw her into the cot, and yelled at her to keep quiet, or I'd . . .'

She drew in her breath, closing her eyes tightly against the tears, seeing herself standing at the foot of the cot, screaming abuse and threats at a helpless, howling baby.

'*Oh, God*, I hated myself!' she said. 'I could see what I was doing, as though I was some other person, watching it all, and I couldn't stop. It was . . . you can't imagine how awful it was. I told her if she didn't shut up, I'd hit her . . . and I would have, I was so close to doing it . . . and I knew I had to get out before I did. I wasn't safe to stay with her . . .' Her breath shuddered into her lungs. 'Oh, Drew!' she said, her voice filled with horror and self-loathing. 'Can you understand? She wasn't safe with me! I was just like my mother, after all!'

He held her closely while she cried out the grief and shame, the pain and terror. When she was finally quiet, lying against him exhausted by emotion, he said quietly, 'What do you mean, like your mother?'

'They took me away from her,' she said, her voice drained of emotion. 'Because of what she did to me.'

'Oh, my God!' he breathed. His eyes found the almost invisible old scars that she had never explained to him, and returned to hers with a new, painful comprehension. 'Karen—I wish you'd told me. You would never discuss those scars—and I never guessed it was anything like that. And I thought your childhood had spoiled you rotten. How wrong could I be? You being hurt—and terrorised, I suppose, by your own mother ...'

'I hardly remember, and I think that I loved her ... I missed her a lot at first, I used to cry for her at night ... but I know she frightened me ... and I couldn't bear to think that I would ever do that to Holly. But that day ... I realised that I couldn't be trusted not to. They say that it runs from generation to generation. I'd thought I was different, that I was going to be a real mother, a perfect mother, and never lose my temper. That I'd be patient and loving and careful. And instead, I was a danger to my own child. That's why I had to go away from her—and from you. I couldn't stay, because I might do something dreadful to her.'

'So you removed yourself, as fast and as far as you could—and for ever, as you thought.'

'Yes.' She drew a long, shuddering breath.

'Didn't you ever look back?' he asked. 'You never once tried to contact me except to offer me a divorce.'

'Several times I almost came back. I wanted to so much, sometimes I didn't think I could stand it. But I knew I daren't. That I couldn't risk it happening to Holly, as it had to me.' She paused, her eyes closed against what she was afraid of seeing in his. 'I don't blame you if you despise me, Drew. I hated myself for a long time. You've been a much better parent for her than I was.'

'Ssh,' he said, stroking her hair. 'I haven't.'

'Yes, you ...'

'Karen ... I've barely stopped myself from hitting and yelling sometimes, too. I know how you felt. *Believe* me!'

She found that difficult. Drew losing his temper with

Holly? How could he know what demon had possessed her that day? 'You . . . do?' She didn't dare to look at him.

'I do,' he assured her softly. 'Truly. I may not have got to the point that you did . . . quite. But I know what it's like to be nearly there. I suppose I thought it was because I was male and a solo father . . . it never occurred to me that you might have felt the same. That being a woman didn't make you a perfect parent. I guess men still have the feeling that women are automatically better at it than we are. And you never hinted . . . You seemed to be a natural mother . . . and I know you wanted her . . . not so soon, perhaps, but she was wanted, welcomed, loved . . .'

'That doesn't have anything to do with it,' Karen protested vehemently. 'Of course I loved her!'

'I know, I know. But loving a demanding little child takes it out of you. I know that, now. Only I never realised what you were going through. I wish you had told me how bad it was.'

'It wasn't bad all the time. Sometimes it was lovely, everything I'd dreamed about. Only I wasn't able to be a good mother, Holly needed something that I couldn't give . . . I didn't even know what . . . that day frightened me so badly, when I thought I had lost control completely . . . I couldn't risk it, for Holly's sake. And you would never have forgiven me. I don't know which would be worse, knowing that I had hurt her, or having you turn against me . . . condemn me.'

'So instead, you condemned yourself? Darling, why couldn't you have trusted me? If only you'd stayed . . . talked to me . . . I do understand, you know.'

She lifted her head. 'But would you have . . . then?' she asked shrewdly. 'You do now, because you say you've felt the same. But at that time, when you didn't know what it's like to have a tiny child depending on you, and not being able to do what you feel you ought to be able to do for her ... I don't know if you would have been shocked and repelled instead of sympathetic.'

There was a long silence. At last she felt his chest rise and fall in a short sigh. 'Maybe. I guess I can't say for sure what my reactions would have been then. But I wish you'd given me the chance, not just gone on pretending you were coping all right until it got to where you felt you had to get out completely, or break. I can't help thinking that in some way you meant to punish me for what you must have seen as indifference.'

'No, I didn't!'

'Not consciously, I know, but deep down, maybe you resented my preoccupation with getting ahead, my neglect of you and the baby. I was just going blindly on, assuming everything was OK because you kept telling me it was. Because I wanted it to be, I suppose. I should have seen that you needed me.'

'It wasn't your fault. If I had been more mature, perhaps ... but maybe I'm just an inadequate sort of person. Other mothers cope without beating their babies.'

'You're not inadequate,' he said. 'You're incredibly strong and brave. You have tremendous will-power, doing what you did. But I wish you'd talked to me, instead of just walking away like that.'

'I couldn't, I was too ashamed. I felt like a criminal, or worse. I still feel appallingly guilty. I don't think I can ever forgive myself.' She pushed away from him suddenly, in a wild panic. '*Promise* you won't ever tell Holly!'

'I think Holly may have more understanding than you give her credit for. It may help her, if she ever has children herself, if you could ... talk to her about it.'

Rejection showed in her face. But perhaps he was right. 'I'll think about it,' she said.

'She says she wants half a dozen kids. She's nuts about babies. Comes of being an only child, I suppose.'

Karen stiffened, and he put a finger on her lips, saying swiftly, 'That wasn't a hint.'

'I know.' She buried her face in his shoulder and said, her voice muffled, 'I'm scared, Drew.'

'I realise that. Don't worry about it. No one's insisting.'

'You want it though ... another baby.'

'Not as much as I want you to be happy. For what it's worth, I'd never leave you to cope on your own again, the way I did before.'

'I've sometimes had this mad wish that I could try all over again, be a decent mother ...'

'You don't have to prove anything. You haven't done anything you need to be ashamed of, darling. And I know that you never will. Not just because next time, if there is one, I'll be supporting you all the way, but because you're strong, and loving, and capable. Only remember, no one expects you to be perfect all the time. It seems to me you simply asked too much of yourself. If you'd admitted earlier that you were overworked and irritable and exhausted, and demanded some help from me, you wouldn't have got to the stage that you did, in the end. I won't let you get into a state like that again.'

It was her turn to be silent. 'I'd like ... to think about it,' she said finally. 'It's tempting, but rather frightening. I do love you, Drew.'

His arms about her tightened. 'That's what really hurt,' he said roughly. 'I thought you didn't. That in spite of what we had shared, in spite of Holly, you'd left me. I knew how much you loved her ... so I figured it was me you really couldn't stand to be with. Or at least, that it wasn't worth giving up the luxuries you were used to, just to be with me. When I saw you again, I was so angry. I was even angry when I first offered to let you see her. I'd realised that you cared for her, that day that you hurt yourself. I'll never forget the look in your eyes when you asked how she was, and I slammed you down—if I'd hit you, you couldn't have looked more stricken. Feeling like that, I just knew you had a right to see her, and at the same time I was furious with myself for offering you the chance. I told myself it would serve you right if you never saw her at all. And then you said no. And I was even more furious with you. I kept telling myself you were a selfish, heartless bitch. And yet I wanted you so much. I pretended it was for Holly's sake that I offered you contact with her. But deep down, I knew that I just couldn't face the thought of losing you all over again. That's why I made sure you saw her. Because I knew she was a bait you couldn't resist.'

'I knew you couldn't have come into the shop by chance.'

'Of course not. It was mad, a crazy impulse that hit me when we were shopping for her birthday present. She hadn't seen anything she liked, and I thought, why not? I'll take her in there, Karen will see her, and ...'

'And?'

'I don't know. I guess I just felt that if you saw her, you wouldn't be able to walk away again.'

'You were right. At the time I thought you were being cruel. I'd spent years trying to forget, trying to fight the urge to see her—and you. Once I bought tickets ... I was half-way home, before I turned back. Because I thought, even if I was more mature, more able to cope, you wouldn't want me back. You would have made a life without me, and I had no right to barge back into it and complicate things for you ... and Holly. And then, when you brought her into the shop ... there you were, and there she was ... I thought you were doing it to punish me, to let me see her and not be able to ... to have her. Like showing food to a starving man, and not letting him eat it. I never thought that you'd want me back, after what I did.'

'I wanted you,' he said. 'Desperately. I've always wanted you, from the very first time I saw you. I've always loved you. Nothing you did could ever alter that.'

'I always felt you'd been trapped into marrying me,' she said. 'I wasn't sure if it was really love at all.'

'Nothing else,' he assured her, stroking her hair back from her face so that he could kiss her warm, throbbing mouth. 'Nothing else then, now, and always.'

She said his name, and linked her arms about his neck, her whole body languid with a mixture of overwhelming relief and love and gratitude. For the first time in ten years she was totally and utterly at peace, and the feeling was blissful. 'I love you so much,' she murmured against his mouth. 'I was horribly afraid that if I told you the truth, you'd be so disgusted, you'd send me away again.'

'Never. I could never send you away. Don't ever leave me again.'

She shook her head. 'This time is for ever, Drew.'

'Yes, my darling. This time is for ever.'

Coming in April

Harlequin Category Romance Specials!

Look for six new and exciting titles from this mix of two genres.

4 Regencies—lighthearted romances set in England's Regency period (1811-1820)

2 Gothics—romance plus suspense, drama and adventure

Regencies

Daughters Four by Dixie Lee McKeone
She set out to matchmake for her sister, but reckoned without the Earl of Beresford's devilish sense of humor.

Contrary Lovers by Clarice Peters
A secret marriage contract bound her to the most interfering man she'd ever met!

Miss Dalrymple's Virtue by Margaret Westhaven
She needed a wealthy patron—and set out to buy one with the only thing she had of value....

The Parson's Pleasure by Patricia Wynn
Fate was cruel, showing her the ideal man, then making it impossible for her to have him....

Gothics

Shadow over Bright Star by Irene M. Pascoe
Did he want her shares to the silver mine, her love—or her life?

Secret at Orient Point by Patricia Werner
They seemed destined for tragedy despite the attraction between them....

CAT88A-1

The passionate saga
that began with SARAH continues in the compelling,
unforgettable story of

Elizabeth

MAURA SEGER

In the aftermath of the Civil War, a divided nation—and two
tempestuous hearts—struggle to become one.

Harlequin Intrigue
Adopts a New Cover Story!

**We are proud to present to you
the new Harlequin Intrigue cover design.**

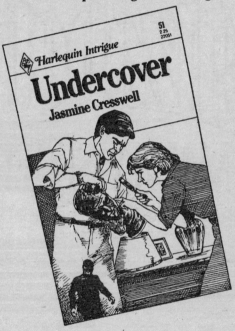

Look for two exciting new stories each month, which mix a contemporary, sophisticated romance with the surprising twists and turns of a puzzler . . . romance with "something more."

CAROLE MORTIMER

JUST ONE NIGHT

Hawk Sinclair—Texas millionaire and owner of the exclusive
Sinclair hotels, determined to protect his son's inheritance.
Leonie Spencer—desperate to protect her sister's happiness.

They were together for just one night.
The night their daughter was conceived.

Blackmail, kidnapping and attempted murder add suspense
to passion in this exciting bestseller.

The success story of Carole Mortimer continues with *Just
One Night*, a captivating romance from the author of the
bestselling novels, *Gypsy* and *Merlyn's Magic*.

★

**Available in March
wherever paperbacks are sold.**

WTCH-1